Knowsley Libra~

Please return ~ *or*
before the ~ *below*

Knowsley Council

Joe pulled her close again and they crossed the street to her house.

She handed him the key to her door. "You know, I think it's safer for you if I stay at your house until we find Bailey Heath."

He slid her jacket off her shoulders and Laura turned to look at him, smiling. "Oh, yeah? And is some psychopath stalker the only reason you're interested in staying here?"

He hung her jacket on the back of the dining room chair and soon his followed suit. He turned his gaze on her. It could be called nothing less than predatory.

Everything inside her heated at the look in his eyes.

"Are you saying you might be interested in something other than me being your bodyguard?" He took a step closer.

"I'm pretty sure there's something I'd like you to do with my body, but guard it isn't what I had in mind." She gripped the waistband of his jeans and pulled him closer. She took a step back until her spine was fully up against the door.

He was everything she should run from. He was everything she craved.

Chapter One

She'd watched him for a year.

She'd traveled all over the country going wherever he went. Others might call it pathetic, but she didn't think so. Besides, what else did she have to do since he'd taken everything from her?

Joe Matarazzo had cost her the man she'd loved. Losing everything after that—her job, her friends, her home—had been his fault, too. Joe Matarazzo had cost her the future.

So now she journeyed around and watched him. Or when she couldn't travel she scoured the internet for information about him.

Whenever she heard his name on a police

scanner she prepared to rush to the scene. She had no doubt he would save the day once again.

Why couldn't he have saved the day when it had mattered the most?

Fire had taken the man she loved. Joe Matarazzo could have stopped it, but he hadn't. Hadn't tried hard enough, not like he would today. Not like how hard she'd seen him try in all his other successful situations. He had the most important job: rescuing those who couldn't rescue themselves. Leading them to safety. Putting their lives before his own.

But he hadn't done his job a year ago. Almost exactly a year ago now. On that day he hadn't tried hard enough. Hadn't cared enough about those he tried to help.

Since that time she had observed him, followed him, studied him. She knew everything about him. Because of that, she could say with a clear conscience that he was guilty.

The time had come for Joe Matarazzo to

atone for his wrongdoings. To suffer for the lives he'd lost.

He'd paid no price for what he'd done. Instead, he had women, he had money, he had everything. But soon that would change. She would see to it.

First, Joe would fall. And as he did, he would know the pain of losing what he cared about most.

Then he would burn.

Just like the fire that had taken her love.

"CASANOVA HAS STRUCK AGAIN. I know it's hard, fellas—don't be jealous just because Joe Matarazzo looks better on your girl than her outfit."

Joe rolled his eyes and tried to snatch the newspaper clipping out of Derek Waterman's—Joe's Omega Sector Critical Response Division colleague—hands. Derek shifted slightly, holding the paper just beyond Joe's reach since they were both strapped into the bench seat of the twin-engine helicopter.

Who even read a physical newspaper anymore? Joe hadn't looked at a news report that wasn't on his smartphone or computer for years. Not that his dating life was *news*, print version or otherwise.

Joe had no idea why so many people would want to read about his love life. Yeah, his family had money—a lot of it—and yeah, he'd grown up with some Hollywood A-listers and ended up photographed a lot.

And yeah—he grinned just a little, glancing out the helicopter's window as Derek continued to read and the seventy miles between Colorado Springs and Denver whirled past—Joe tended to be a bit of a bad boy. Had a reputation with the ladies.

So what? He liked women.

"The lady du jour was Natasha Suzanne Bleat, daughter of British diplomat Marcus Bleat…"

Joe tuned out as Derek read Natasha's impressive list of family credentials through the headphones that allowed all of them to communicate with each other. Jon Hatton and Lillian Muir—the first an Omega profiler and the second Omega SWAT like Derek—listened raptly from the pilot and copilot seats where Lillian controlled the aircraft.

Seriously, Joe's colleagues loved this stuff, ridiculous as it may be. They had a whole scrapbook full of Joe's clippings.

Joe had grown up with press and had learned to pretty much ignore it. The press had their own agenda and nobody's best interests in mind but theirs. He learned that lesson a little too late, but learned it.

And it wasn't like paparazzi followed him around. Yet for whatever reason, gossip sites and society pages loved to report on his dating life. A dating life he had to admit was pretty extensive. Everyone called him Casanova. The press and even his colleagues at Omega.

Joe wasn't offended. It took a hell of a lot more to offend him.

"...the redhead beauty was last seen entering the Los Angeles Four Seasons with Joe, arm in arm."

Joe raised his gaze heavenward with a long-suffering sigh and waited for the rest, but that was it.

"Last seen?" Joe finally succeeded in snatching the paper away from Derek. "They make it sound like I killed her and hid her body."

"Oh, it sounds like you did something to her body, but I don't think anyone figures you killed her. At least not literally." Lillian snickered from her pilot's seat.

"I have no idea how you get so lucky, dude." Derek closed his eyes and leaned farther back on the bench seat next to Joe. "No matter what city we're in, the women throw themselves at you."

Joe could've pointed out that speeding their way to a hostage negotiation scene was probably not the time to discuss the press version of his love life. But he knew this sort of distraction helped keep the team loose and relaxed.

There would be plenty of time for tension and focus when they landed and assessed the scene.

Joe shrugged. "What can I say? I'm #blessed, man." He made the hashtag symbol with his hands, tapping his fingers together.

Everyone groaned.

"Don't make me shoot you. I'd catch flack for shooting an unarmed man." Derek didn't open his eyes as he said it.

Joe was the only unarmed person in the helicopter. Although he was trained in the use of a number of weapons, he almost always went into situations unarmed.

He was Omega Sector's top hostage negotiator. And he was damn good at his job.

Joseph Gregory Terrance Matarazzo III didn't

need a career. At least, didn't need one for a salary. He'd been born with money, had known its benefits his entire life. Had used those benefits for a carefree, fun-loving existence until about six years ago when he'd turned twenty-five and decided maybe he'd like to do something with his time besides sit around and look good.

The laid-back, playboy, slacker and media darling had decided to become a better man.

Joe had skills. Not the same skills Derek had in his ability to formulate the best tactical advantage in any given hostile situation. Or the ones Lillian had with the many ways she could kill someone not only through the use of weapons, but just her scary, tiny, bare hands. Or Hatton with whatever he did, which was pretty much overthink everything and come up with scenarios and means of handling crises.

Joe's skills rested with people. He had a charming way with others. He knew it. Everybody knew it. Joe excelled at talking to people,

To Allison, my editor.
You gave me my first shot
and I'll forever be grateful. Here
we are, ten books later, and you still
haven't gotten a restraining order
against me yet. I'll consider that a win.
Thank you for all you do.

Janie Crouch has loved to read romance her whole life. She cut her teeth on Mills & Boon Romance novels as a preteen, then moved on to a passion for romantic suspense as an adult. Janie lives with her husband and four children overseas. She enjoys traveling, long-distance running, watching movies, knitting and adventure/obstacle racing. You can find out more about her at janiecrouch.com.

First Published in Great Britain 2016
By Mills & Boon, an imprint of HarperCollins*Publishers*
1 London Bridge Street, London, SE1 9GF

Large Print edition 2017
© 2016 Janie Crouch
ISBN: 978-0-263-07223-5

Our policy is to use papers that are natural, renewable and recyclable products and made from wood grown in sustainable forests. The logging and manufacturing processes conform to the legal environmental regulations of the country of origin.

Printed and bound in Great Britain
by CPI Antony Rowe, Chippenham, Wiltshire

Overwhelming Force

JANIE CROUCH

listening to them, making them feel comfortable. He was likable, a cool kid. The type of person people wanted to be around.

It wasn't an act. Joe honestly cared about people, even the hostage-takers he was sent to talk to. So he tried his damnedest to connect with the people in these situations, to listen to them and see what he could do so everyone could leave the situation alive. If Joe did his job right, nobody had to get hurt.

If he didn't do his job right, the Dereks and Lillians with the guns came in with a different solution.

Most of the time Joe successfully completed his mission and nobody was harmed. Sometimes there was no other way and the bad guys got wounded or worse. Joe was trained—and wasn't hesitant—to make the hard call when he knew he wasn't going to be able to neutralize the situation and SWAT needed to step in and take the

tangos out. That situation wasn't Joe's prefer-
ence, but he didn't lose sleep when it happened.

Every once in a while something went terribly
wrong and innocent people got hurt. Joe touched
a burn scar at the base of his neck, one that continued over his shoulder and partway down his
back. Innocent people had been hurt that day a
year ago. Innocent people had died.

Joe planned to use his skills today to make
sure another situation like that didn't happen
again.

Derek and Jon began arguing over the name
of the woman the press had spotted Joe with a
few days before Natasha during an Omega case
in Austin, Texas.

"Her name was Kerri. I'm telling you." Jon's
voice came crisply through the headphones.
"Kerri with an *i*. I remember it clear as day."

"No," Derek said. "That was the one before.
Austin was Kelli. But also with an *i*."

Joe wondered what Derek's brilliant wife,

Molly, the crime lab director at Omega, and Jon's fiancée, Sherry Mitchell, a hugely talented forensic artist, would have to say about their men's topic of conversation.

No doubt they would find it as ridiculous as Joe did.

Joe remembered both Kerri and Kelli. He'd had dinner with one, a drink at a bar with the other. Nothing more. Just like the night at the hotel with Natasha when Joe had walked her, admittedly arm in arm, to her room. And left her there.

Because, hell, nobody could be as much of a Casanova as the press wanted to label him. God knew he wasn't a monk, but sometimes the women he was with were just pleasant company—clothes *on*—and nothing more.

But Joe hated to deny his colleagues their fun.

"Would you like me to settle this, boys?" he asked, sighing.

"For the love of all that is holy, please yes,

Matarazzo, settle this." Lillian's higher voice cut through the baritone of the three men.

"You're both wrong. It was Kerri *and* Kelli. Both of them in Austin. *Together.*" Joe smiled as he told the lie.

If they wanted Casanova he would give it to them. He knew he probably shouldn't since it reinforced what his colleagues already thought to be the truth about him: that he was less part of the Omega team and more like a novelty. But Joe was great at figuring out what people needed and becoming that, at least for a little while. A distraction en route to a troublesome situation? No problem.

Hatton and Derek both groaned, neither knowing whether to believe him.

"I'm going to check some of the gossip sites when I get back to HQ," Hatton threatened.

"You do that," Joe responded. "Because you know everything they publish can be taken as gospel."

Silence fell as they flew the last few miles and Lillian landed the helicopter on the roof helipad of a building that had been cleared two blocks from First National Bank of South Denver. Temporary home of two bad guys and a dozen or so hostages.

Lillian landed and switched off the rotors. "Time to go to work, boys."

Joe slid the door open and he and Derek both ducked their heads and briskly made their way down the stairs, out of the building and over to the bank. Jon quickly joined them as they found the officer in charge. Lillian would be there after she took care of the helicopter. Jokes and talk about Joe's exploits ceased. Omega now had a job to do.

The older man shook everyone's hand. "I'm Sheriff Richardson. We appreciate you coming out so quickly."

"We need the most up-to-date intel you have," Derek told the sheriff. Joe was glad the locals had called Omega and egos hadn't come into play. Situations like this tended to be delicate enough without law enforcement working against each other.

Richardson nodded. "We have two men in their midtwenties holding, as best as we can tell, sixteen people hostage inside the bank. Two of those hostages are children. They've been inside for two hours and we haven't been able to speak with them, despite trying multiple times."

Richardson turned from Derek to Joe. "You're the negotiator, right? The city has a good one of our own, but she had a baby a couple of days ago. She was still going to come in but I put a stop to that immediately."

Joe nodded. "That was the right decision. I won't let you down, Sheriff. I'll do my very best to get everyone out safely."

"Do you have building plans for the bank, Sheriff?" Derek asked.

"Yes." He gestured over to a younger man who

brought them over. Lillian joined them, and she, Derek and Hatton were soon poring over the plans.

Joe took a deep breath, looking out at the small bank. He couldn't see anything happening inside. The Denver County police didn't have a sizable SWAT team, but it did appear like they had a couple of marksmen. He knew Derek and Lillian were both expert sharpshooters also.

He hoped it wouldn't come to that.

Why were the hostage-takers here at this particular bank? Had they tried to rob it then got stuck so took hostages? Robbing a bank wasn't a very smart move and didn't have a high success rate, but people did desperate things sometimes.

There were kids inside. That upped the ante a lot. Joe's natural inclination was to march up to the door right now, even without backup. But he knew to set wheels in motion before Derek and the team were ready could spell disaster for everyone.

"Derek, there are kids, man," Joe said softly. He knew he didn't have to remind his friend of that—with his pregnant wife, it would be in the forefront of Derek's mind, too—but couldn't help himself. "They've already been in there a long time. Let me know which direction you'll be coming from if it goes south and I'll get started. At least get the kids out."

"There's not a lot of good options with a bank this old that was built in the fifties," Derek muttered, studying the plans more intently. "It looks like the roof will be our best bet. Probably a ventilation shaft. We might have to send Lillian through alone if it's too small."

Lillian alone would be plenty enough to put down two tangos. Joe nodded at her; she winked at him. Despite her beauty, he had never tried to make a move on her. He knew better than to hit on a woman who made a living shooting people.

"Okay," Joe said. "What's today's go-signal?"

The team always had a phrase and action, both

meant only to be used as a last resort, that Joe could use to signal SWAT that the situation inside was out of hand and they needed to use deadly force.

"Word is *sunglasses*." Derek glanced up from the plans. "Action is putting your sunglasses on your head."

Joe's shades were in the pocket of his shirt. Unlike the other Omega members, all wearing full combat gear and bulletproof vests, Joe was wearing a black T-shirt, jeans and casual brown boots. It was important that he seem as normal and nonthreatening as possible when he approached the hostage-takers.

"Be careful in there, Joe." It was Jon who looked up from the building plans this time. "We've got a lot of blinds here. I know you're good on the fly, but watch your six."

Joe nodded, already beginning to walk toward the building. "Those kids and their mother will be coming out first. Be ready for them."

He blew out a breath through gritted teeth, forcing his shoulders then jaw to relax. Coming in tense—or at least looking overly tense—never helped. There were two guys in there who needed to be heard. Joe wanted to do that. But even more he wanted to get the hostages out safely. Every one of them.

Joe walked up to the glass door of the bank and knocked, then held his hands up in a position of surrender so they could see he wasn't armed. And he waited.

He was about to become best buddies with two potentially dangerous guys.

Just another day at the office for Joe Matarazzo.

Chapter Two

Laura Birchwood should've sent her assistant to the bank to get these stupid papers signed.

But *no*, Laura had wanted to get out of the office, get some nice fresh air on this relatively warm, sunny April day in Colorado. It had been a long, cold winter and it had snowed even as late as a week and a half ago.

So when it had been in the upper 60s on a late Friday afternoon and her Colorado Springs law office—Coach, Birchwood and Winchley, LLP—had needed the signature of a bank manger here on the outskirts of Denver, Laura had offered to make the trip herself. Her assistant had Friday night plans; Laura didn't. Laura decided she would have dinner in Denver while she was here. She'd be by herself, but that wasn't anything unusual.

The two guys pacing frantically with big guns, stopping every once in a while to wave them around and scare the people sitting on the bank floor, were going to ruin her dinner plans.

As pathetic as the plans were.

Laura refused to let herself panic, even when the guys glanced over in her direction. Hysteria wasn't going to help anything in this situation; as a matter of fact, she was pretty sure the hostage-takers would just feed off it and become more aggravated.

"I have to get them out of here," Brooke, the young mother sitting next to Laura, whispered. "They're going to get hungry soon. Get upset."

She referred to the two girls the mom had with her, a baby maybe eight or nine months, not old enough yet to be crawling, thank goodness, and a five-year-old. Both had done remarkably well so far. Brooke herself had done great. She'd fed the baby a bottle and given the older girl, Samantha, a box of crayons and a coloring book she'd had in her diaper bag.

Most of all she'd stayed calm. Her daughters had picked up on their mother's cues and had also stayed calm. Laura wasn't even sure Samantha really understood what was happening.

"Police will be coming, Brooke," Laura whispered to her. "I have a packet of peanut butter crackers in my purse for Samantha. That will buy us some time."

"I need to make another bottle." Brooke gestured to the baby currently sitting in her lap, playing with some teething toys. "And I know her diaper is wet. I'm going to have to talk to them."

"No, I'll talk to them—"

Laura flinched as one of the two men, the loud

one, let out a loud string of obscenities. "Shut up over there!" he yelled, pacing more wildly.

Samantha looked up from her coloring. "He said a bad word," she whispered to Laura.

He'd said a bunch of them. Laura wasn't sure which one the girl meant.

"You're not supposed to say *shut up*," Samantha stated primly, then went back to her coloring.

Laura couldn't help but smile. It was nice to meet a kid whose definition of foul language revolved around the words *shut up*.

She had to get Brooke and her two beautiful daughters out of here. She knew drawing the men's attention to her by asking them to release Brooke and the girls could be dangerous. Laura had no idea what the men wanted. To be honest she wasn't even sure these men knew exactly what they wanted.

The local police had tried calling the bank. The men had made the employees unplug all the phones and then had hit the assistant manager on the head with their gun. The man was conscious but still had blood oozing down the side of his face. They'd forced everyone to put their cell phones in a trash can and placed it in the middle of the room.

If the robbers decided to start killing hostages, Laura didn't want to put herself at the front of the line. But she sure as hell wasn't going to let Brooke do it. And now that there was no way the police could contact the men to see what they wanted, Laura didn't know how the police could help.

She reached over and squeezed Brooke's hand.

"Laura, wait, don't—"

Laura was standing up when a knock on the bank's front door suddenly drew everyone's attention. She didn't have a good angle to take in the whole scene but could see the upheld arms of a man standing there. She quickly sat back down.

The robbers went ballistic.

"Who are you? What do you want?" one screamed at the person at the door, voice shrill.

"We'll kill everyone in here. Every last one of them. Get away!"

The man outside didn't move except to gesture to them to unlock the door.

The two men began frantically talking between themselves. Laura couldn't hear all of it, but knew one of the men at least understood that the man at the door was a hostage negotiator.

Hopefully the guy was a good one.

Finally the two men broke apart from their huddle. The negotiator was still standing arms upstretched by the entrance. Laura still couldn't see his face.

"You." One of the hostage-takers pointed over to the bank manager. "Get over here and open the door."

The manager got shakily to his feet and walked to the door gathering a large ring of keys from his pocket. The robber got behind him, using the man as a human shield, and put the gun directly to the manager's temple.

The baby started fussing and Laura reached over to hold her so Brooke could get out another bottle. Plus, if bullets started flying Brooke could grab Samantha and Laura could try to protect the baby.

"You better pray that this guy doesn't try anything. Because you'll be dead before you hit the floor if he does. Open it just a crack," the man holding the manager said.

The manager nodded as he put the key in the door. Rivers of sweat rolled down his face. The room remained silent.

"P-please don't do anything," the manager said to the man outside. "He'll kill me if you do anything."

"Nah, no plans to do anything to make anybody nervous." The negotiator's voice was clear and friendly. And oddly familiar to Laura. "I swear to you all, I am unarmed and just here to talk. To see what we can work out. To find a solution where all of us get out of here without getting hurt."

"How do I know you're not armed?" the robber yelled from behind the manager, keeping his head down.

"I'm going to reach down now and lift up my shirt and turn around. You'll see. No weapon at all. No earpiece. Nothing."

She still couldn't see his face, but Laura and the rest of the bank were treated to the sight of rock-solid abs as the man lifted his shirt and turned around slowly. Under any other circumstances Laura would've just enjoyed the view.

"You could have a gun in your pants," the other man said. "An ankle holster or something. We're not stupid."

"No, you're right. You're smart to think of that. Most people wouldn't."

The negotiator was good. He'd already tuned in to what the robbers needed to hear: that they were smart, in control. The man ripped off his shirt and dropped it to the ground.

"I'm going to take off my jeans, okay? Not trying to give anyone a show, but you're smart to check and make sure I really don't have any weapons."

Strong muscular legs came into view as the man kicked off his boots and socks and then took off his jeans. Black boxer briefs were all that was left on the negotiator. Laura sort of hoped the robbers would let him in, not only so he could negotiate them out of this mess, but so she could see his face. Would it be as impressive as the rest of him?

"Miss Laura—" Samantha giggled "—that man only has his underwear on."

Laura smiled. "I know, sweetie. He's silly." She bounced the baby on her legs, thankful she wasn't crying anymore.

"So as you can see," the negotiator continued, "no weapons. Well, *one*, if you know what I mean. But I generally only bring that one out for the ladies." Laura could hear the smile in his voice. "Do you mind if I come in and talk? It's a nice day but still a little chilly out here in just my drawers."

"Fine," the guy behind the bank manager finally said. "Get in here. But if you do anything suspicious at all, I'll start killing people."

The guy grabbed his pile of clothes and quickly squeezed through the door. The manager relocked it and the bad guy got away from the danger of the door and pointed his gun at the negotiator.

Laura could feel her jaw literally drop when she got her first full look at him.

Standing there in his boxer briefs was Joe Matarazzo.

She never thought she would see him again. Had *hoped* she would never see him again. And now it looked like her life was in his hands.

Just went to prove that behind every worst-case scenario, there was a *worse* worst-case scenario.

JOE KNEW HE would never hear the end of this little striptease from his Omega colleagues. But he'd been certain he couldn't get into the bank any other way. These two guys were paranoid, frantic. Joe knew immediately he needed to put himself in a position of seeming to be the beta. Let them feel like they were alpha.

Joe's pride, his true feelings, his personality, didn't matter. All that mattered was getting everyone out of the bank safely.

If they had asked him to take off his boxers, he would've done that, too. But he was glad they hadn't.

Joe quickly assessed one half of the bank as he put his jeans back on. The bank manager seemed scared to death and had some bruising on the side of his face—probably took a punch—but otherwise appeared fine. An injured man, also a bank employee, sat propped up against the wall. Looked like he also had received a blow to the side of the face. Bloody, but not life-threatening.

All the bank employees being alive was a good sign. It meant these two guys probably didn't want to hurt anyone. Probably had planned to rob the bank and things had escalated.

No one was dead yet, so that meant there was a very good chance that Joe could get everyone out unharmed.

"I'm Joe, by the way," he told the two men as he pulled his shirt back over his head.

"You expect us to tell you our names so you can get a bunch of information on us? No way, man." Both men had their weapons aimed directly at Joe.

Joe wanted to point out the flaws in their logic: how was he supposed to get any information? He'd just gotten almost naked in front of them so they knew he didn't have any communication devices. And even if he did, what would a bunch of information do versus two very real guns?

But pointing out the logic flaws would only put them more on the defensive.

"No, nothing like that. I was just wondering what to call you."

"You can call me Ricky and him Bobby," the older of the two men said, sneering.

Joe recognized Ricky Bobby. "Yeah, I saw that movie." Joe smiled. "The kids, Walker and Texas Ranger. Hilarious. *Anchorman* was my favorite though."

The men's weapons lowered just the slightest bit. Good. Just keep them thinking about Will Ferrell and movies. Based on their coloring and size, Joe guessed Ricky and Bobby to be brothers.

He turned casually in the opposite direction so he could see the other half of the bank as he crouched down to put his shoes back on.

There were the kids. Good. A little girl alternating between coloring and watching what was going on and a baby in her mom's lap. Joe glanced at the mom's face to see how she was holding up.

And found the angry eyes of Laura Birchwood.

Joe felt the air leave his lungs.

Man, she hadn't changed at all in the six years since he'd seen her, well, except for the two kids part. She still had wavy brown hair and a face more interesting than it was traditionally pretty. But it was still the face he'd never been able to ever get out of his mind.

The pain that assaulted him at the knowledge that Laura had moved on so completely from him took him by surprise. She obviously had found herself a husband and had a couple of kids, given the cute little baby who bounced on her knees.

After what he'd said to her when their relationship ended, Joe couldn't blame her for moving on. It still hurt like hell though.

Joe stood from putting on his boots and looked at the two men. He needed to focus.

"Ricky, Bobby, I want to help you guys. They sent me in here to figure out what we can do to work this out peaceful-like." He carefully didn't use the word *cops* in case that was some sort of trigger word for the two men "There's nothing that has been done here yet that makes the situation terrible. You guys and I can walk out of here right now and everything can be made right."

That wasn't totally accurate. Ricky and Bobby would be doing some jail time for this little stunt. But it would be much worse if they killed someone. Joe didn't really think they were just going to walk out with him, but it was worth a shot.

"No," Ricky said. "They'll shoot us as soon as we come out. Or at least arrest us."

"Nobody wants to shoot you. I promise you that," Joe quickly interjected. He needed to keep the level of paranoia as low as possible.

"Well, we're not going out there. Not until we

have what we need." Bobby looked over at the bank manager.

Okay, so they did want something. Probably money. That was good, something Joe could work with, something he could talk to them about.

Something that provided him leverage.

"That sounds reasonable. Is what you need going to hurt anybody?"

If what they needed was to blow up a bank full of people while the press was watching to make some sort of political or religious statement, then it was going to be time for Joe to pull out the sunglasses to signal SWAT awfully quick. But Ricky and Bobby didn't seem to be the political statement types.

"No," Bobby said. "What we want is ours. We just want it back."

To the side, Joe heard Laura's baby start to cry. He needed to get her and the children out of here. Right now. He couldn't stand the thought of Laura being hurt again. Or especially her innocent children.

Joe had hurt her enough once. Maybe he could begin to make that right by getting her and her family out of danger.

"Alright, I can do that. That's why I was sent in here. To see what it is you need and help find a way to get it for you. That's my only job here, figuring out a way this can end okay for everyone."

Again, that wasn't actually true, but the baby's cries were getting louder. Ricky and Bobby both turned to glare at the child and Joe briefly thought of trying to take both of them down physically himself, but he decided not to risk it. Somebody might get hurt. Plus, it was too early in the negotiation process. If Joe broke their trust now, he would not get it back.

"She's got to shut that kid up," Bobby told Ricky.

"Listen, guys…" Joe took a small step closer

so they would turn their attention—and weapons—back on him and away from Laura's side of the room. "I think we can solve a couple of problems here with one action."

"What are you talking about?" Bobby's eyes narrowed.

"Like you said, that baby is a huge headache. Plus the people outside—" Joe again was careful not to call them *law enforcement* or *police* "—would take it as a sign of good faith if you let the kids and their mom go. Works for everyone. You get rid of a screaming baby, and the people outside know you're reasonable. Win/win. You've still got plenty of people left in here for whatever you need to do."

Bobby looked over at his older brother and Ricky finally nodded. Joe felt like a hundred-pound weight had been lifted off his chest. Now, no matter what happened, at least Laura and her kids would be safe.

Keeping his eyes on Ricky and Bobby, Joe motioned for Laura and the kids to come over.

"Get the manager to open the door again," Ricky told him, so Joe turned to the man. The heavyset manager got to his feet and moved to the door.

Joe turned back to reassure Laura as best he could but found another woman taking the baby from her. Clutching the infant in one arm and holding the hand of the little girl in the other, she made her way to Joe.

"You're their mom?" Joe asked. "I thought the other lady was holding the baby."

"She was just helping me," the woman whispered. "Thank you for getting us out."

Joe squeezed her shoulder. "When the door opens, walk straight across the street. Don't stop for anything."

The woman nodded.

"Okay, are we ready?" he asked.

Joe turned to Ricky and Bobby and fought

back a shudder when he saw that Bobby now had Laura held right in front of him in a choke hold, gun pointed at her temple.

"If anyone does anything I don't like, I'll put a bullet in her," Bobby said.

Joe ground his teeth. It took quite a lot to get him to lose his cool, but he was finding that a gun to Laura's temple did it very quickly. He forced the anger down. He needed to stay calm.

The manager opened the door and Joe watched as the woman sprinted across the street, the little girl doing her best to keep up. They were safe. He squeezed the shoulder of the bank manager as he relocked the door.

"Thank you for not trying to run," Joe said in a low voice. The man could've taken off when the door was open. Could've saved himself at the cost of other lives. Joe had seen it happen before.

"I couldn't let them kill someone else because of me." The manager rubbed his hands down his pant legs. "But I can't give them what they want. I don't have what they need."

Joe's smile suggested a calm he didn't really feel. "We'll work it out."

Joe finally felt like he could breathe again when Bobby had released Laura and she had sat back down against the wall. She didn't seem to be hurt in any way or even too scared.

As a matter of fact her hazel eyes were all but spitting daggers at Joe. She looked like she might grab Bobby's gun and shoot Joe herself.

Joe winced. Guess she hadn't forgiven him for what he'd said to her six years ago.

He didn't blame her. And he had to admit, as much as he wanted Laura safely out of harm's way, his heart had actually leaped in his chest— seriously, he'd *felt* the adrenaline rush through him—when he realized those children belonged to another woman. Not Laura.

It was time to get this situation resolved so he

could move on to more important things. Like talking Laura into dinner with him.

He had a feeling that might take more negotiation skills than even he possessed.

Chapter Three

Joe Matarazzo working in law enforcement. Who would've *ever* figured that would happen? Certainly not Laura.

But she had to admit, he had quite deftly handled the situation in the bank with Ricky and Bobby. They had come there to steal the last remaining copy of their father's will.

Evidently dear old dad had realized what jerks his sons had become and had decided to leave his "fortune" as Ricky and Bobby called it, a sum of just over twelve thousand dollars, to the local 4-H club.

Two grown men had broken into a bank, held

sixteen people—including *children*—hostage, and had threatened to kill them all to get a will. A will that ultimately would only get them twelve thousand dollars if they were successful.

The perfect storm of idiocy.

The bank manger hadn't had the other key. Every safe-deposit box needed two keys and the manager only had one. That's when the problem had escalated. Ricky and Bobby thought they could just come in, show some ID and have the box opened. But not without the second key.

Demanding the manager open it by pointing a gun at his head hadn't changed the situation. He still couldn't open it with only his one key.

Somehow Bobby and Ricky just hadn't understood that. They got loud. Someone called the cops and next thing they knew they had a hostage situation on their hands.

Laura had no idea what would've happened if Joe hadn't shown up and defused the situation.

He'd sat down with the two men and the bank

manager. The manager swore he would open the safe-deposit box if he could, but that the bank had put security measures in place long ago that required two keys. It's what kept managers from being able to walk in at any time and take anything they wanted from the boxes.

Finally Joe was able to make Ricky and Bobby understand that. He'd then helped them figure out where their dead father's key might be. Explained they needed to surrender so they could come back to the bank another time.

That time was going to be after years in prison, and by then the 4-H club was going to have some pretty nice 4-Hing equipment, or whatever a 4-H club used money for, but Joe had left that part out.

Both men had exited with Joe and had been immediately taken into custody. Everyone inside could hear Ricky and Bobby screaming at Joe, claiming he'd lied about being arrested. Joe hadn't lied, he just hadn't announced all the particulars of the truth. As a lawyer, Laura could appreciate the difference.

Cops and medical workers then rushed into the bank to see who needed help. As they tended to people, Laura watched with a sort of amazed detachment as one of the large air-conditioning grates on a wall about ten feet off the ground moved and a small woman, in full combat gear and rifle, eased her way out, hung as far as her arms would allow her, then dropped to the ground.

She'd been there, probably since not long after Joe arrived, silently ready to move in if things had gotten desperate.

But they hadn't, thanks to Joe.

The woman had just made a quiet sweep of the area with her eyes then walked out the front door. Most of the people inside didn't even notice her.

A uniformed police officer entered and made an announcement. "People, I'm Sheriff Richardson. Right now we're just trying to ascertain who is injured. If you have any wounds at all, or feel like you're having any chest pains or anything like that, please let us know so we can get a medic to attend to you immediately."

Laura's chest hurt a little bit, but she was pretty sure that was indigestion caused from seeing Joe again.

"Otherwise we ask that you stay in the immediate area of the bank so we can take your statement. Certainly you are free to go outside and get some fresh air. Also to call anyone you need to let them know you're okay. This event will make the supper-time news, for sure, and you won't want any family worrying about you."

Laura doubted her parents or brother would hear about this back in Huntsville, Alabama, but she would text them anyway and let them know she was okay. She would not mention the fact that Joe Matarazzo had gotten her out of the situation safely. Her dad and brother might catch the first flight to Denver and take Joe out themselves.

They'd have to get in line behind her.

The image of Joe stripped down to his boxers and smiling charmingly at the two hostage-taking morons popped into her head unbidden.

Damn, he still looked good. Nothing about that had changed, not that she would've expected it to. His tall, lithe body was absolutely drool-worthy: broad shoulders, hard abs that all but begged you to run your fingers over them, trim hips that eased down into long, strong legs.

And that face. Crystal blue eyes and strong, sharp cheekbones and a chin that gave strength to a face that would've otherwise been too pretty. Brown hair with natural sandy highlights, straight, a little long with a half curl that always fell over his forehead.

And his smile. Joe Matarazzo had a quick, easy smile for everyone. The man loved to smile, and had gorgeous sensuous lips and perfect teeth to back up his propensity.

His cheeks were clean-shaven now, but Laura knew firsthand how quickly the stubble would grow and exactly how the roughness of his cheeks would feel as he kissed her all over her body.

She stopped the thought immediately. For six years she'd been stopping those types of thoughts immediately. Instead she fast-forwarded to the last memory she'd had of Joe. Him standing outside her apartment and telling her their relationship wasn't going to work anymore.

That he'd liked her and all, and the last couple of months had been great, but that, let's face it, she just wasn't the *caliber* of woman someone like Joe—with his money and connections and good looks and charm—would be in a long-term relationship with.

Mic drop. Matarazzo out.

Laura could make those little jokes now, almost without wincing. Six years ago she'd just wanted to crawl under a rock and die. Joe may not have used those actual words, but basically said she wasn't attractive enough for him. Silly her, she'd thought the fact that they'd always had a delightful time together, had the same quirky sense of humor and wonderful conversations had meant something. For the six months they had dated, Joe had led her to believe that he thought it was true, too. Until he just changed his mind out of the blue and ended it.

Not the caliber of woman...

So no, she was not going to let the sight of Joe Matarazzo in just his skivvies get her hot and bothered.

"Um, ma'am?"

Laura looked over at the young police officer who had evidently been trying to get her attention for a few moments.

"Yes?"

"Were you hurt in any way? Perhaps a head injury?" The young officer looked confused.

The only damage to Laura's head was in her thoughts about Joe. "No, I'm fine. Just reliving the situation. It's a little painful." She didn't state which situation.

"Do you feel up to giving me your statement? Otherwise we can have you come down to the station tomorrow."

Laura shook her head. No, she didn't want to have to come back. She gave the officer her statement, telling how Ricky and Bobby entered while she was finishing a meeting with the bank manager to get his signature on some financial paperwork for a client.

If Laura had just beelined it for the door she wouldn't have gotten caught in the hostage mess at all. But then she thought of Brooke and little Samantha and the baby. Laura had been glad she'd been able to help them.

The officer took down Laura's information and

told her they'd be in touch if they needed anything else, and that she shouldn't hesitate to contact them if she thought of something more she remembered. She was free to go.

Now all she had to do was make it to her car and get away without having to talk to Joe at all. Not that he'd try to talk to her. After all, what was there left to say?

She supposed she could thank him for doing a good job today and getting them all out alive. She'd been especially impressed at how he'd immediately gotten Brooke and her girls out.

Laura was thankful, but she wasn't willing to actually talk to Joe to tell him that. Maybe she could send the sheriff's office a letter with official thanks. Better. More professional.

She stepped out into the brisk April air of Colorado, closing her eyes and breathing it deep into her lungs. She was alive. She was unhurt. She even had the signature she'd originally come to this bank for. Everything was good.

She opened her eyes and found herself staring directly into the gaze of Joe Matarazzo.

The Rockies in all their stark majesty framed the area behind him. The bright cobalt sky made the perfect matching backdrop for the overwhelming force of his gorgeous blue eyes.

It was ridiculous. Like he was something out of a John Denver song or Bob Ross painting.

"Hey, Laura."

And must the deep timbre of his voice match the sexiness of every other part of his being? Of course. Had God realized he'd given an abnormally large chunk of good genes all to one person? Height, charm, good looks and wealth all wrapped up in one sexy package. Seemed unfair.

"Joe." It was all she could manage.

"It's good to see you. I was thrown off guard for a minute when I spotted you in there."

Laura took a slight step back. He was too close. Anything under a mile was probably too close.

"Well, thanks for getting us out." She waved

her arm like she held a wand. "For doing whatever magic you did and working out the situation so no one got hurt."

Joe shrugged. "Just doing my job."

"Wow, a job?" She tried for light laughter, but
it came out tense and brittle. "That's new, right?
I didn't think you would ever need a job."

Joe looked over to the side of the bank where
the press and bystanders had been roped off.
Laura hadn't even realized they were there, but
saw dozens of smartphones recording them. Recording everyone coming out of the bank.

"Let's go around to the side, so everything we
say doesn't end up online." Joe walked away
from the crowd, around a corner, leading Laura
with a gentle hand at the small of her back.

She could feel his hand through her blouse as
if it seared her. That small touch stole her breath.

And pissed her off.

She didn't want to react this way, didn't want
to feel anything when he touched her except

maybe disgust. She stepped away from his hand, glad there was now no one else around to witness any of this.

"How have you been? It's been a long time," he said when they were out of earshot of everyone else.

She just stared at him. She wasn't sure what to say. If this was some sort of police follow-up to make sure she was okay, then that was fine. Otherwise she didn't want to make small talk with him as if they were old friends who had just lost touch.

"Seeing you here, like I said, it sort of threw me," he continued. He shifted a little nervously, but his friendly smile never wavered.

"Well, you did great. You were amazing with Ricky and Bobby."

He rolled his eyes. "Wasn't up against mastermind criminals there, that's for sure."

"They still had guns and could've hurt a lot of people. So I'm glad you were able to get them to surrender. Although they seem pretty mad at you for it."

They stared at each other for long moments. Laura felt the flare of attraction she knew was only one-sided and realized she had to get out of here. All the damage repair she'd done over the last six years was crumbling down in mere minutes in Joe's presence.

She took another step back. "I've got to go. I gave my statement to one of the policemen inside the bank, so he cleared me to leave."

His blue eyes seemed to bore into her. She looked away.

"Laura—"

"It was nice talking to you. Glad you seem to have a job you like. Take care, Joe." There. A reasonable, polite statement.

Now get out.

She took another step back and to the side. Her car was around the other corner, but she'd walk around the entire block out of her way if it meant she could make a clean getaway from Joe.

"Laura, let me take you out to dinner tonight."

"No." She knew she was too abrupt, but reasonable, polite statements seemed beyond her now.

Joe put his large hands out, palms up, in an endearing, entreating manner. "Just to catch up. It's been what, six years? It's great to see you."

She shook her head. "I can't."

"Why?" He took a step closer and she immediately took a step back. She had to keep some sort of physical distance from him. "Are you married? In a relationship?"

"No."

The attraction was still there for her. She didn't want it to be, but it was. Laura had done her best not to think about him for the last six years while also having to admit that the man had shaped her life like no one else. Because of him the whole course of her career and even her thought patterns had changed.

One brief, cruel conversation with him six years ago had made her into the woman she was today.

"Then why?"

Was he really asking this? Couldn't figure it out on his own? "I just can't. There's too much…" She almost said *ugliness*, but that reminded her too much of what he'd said to her that night. "There's too much time and distance between us."

Faster than she would've thought possible his hands whipped out and grabbed both of her wrists. He held them gently but firmly. "There's still a spark between us."

Laura's laugh was bitter, unrecognizable to her. She wasn't a bitter person. Even though Joe's words six years ago had shredded her she'd never let herself become bitter, even toward him.

"Spark was never the problem, at least not

on my end." She wrenched her arms out of his hands. "The fact that you thought I wasn't attractive enough to be in a relationship with you, *that* was the problem."

Chapter Four

Joe watched Laura hurry down the corridor between the bank and the coffee shop next door then round a corner. He wanted to run after her, to stop her, to explain.

To explain what, exactly? That he'd been a jerk six years ago?

Seemed evident she already understood that pretty clearly.

How about that he'd been a fool? That he'd realized long ago how stupid he'd been to let her go? That Laura's honesty, authenticity and love for life had been something he'd missed day in and day out for six years?

Perhaps he could tell her that he'd nearly called her dozens of times. Had stood outside her house in Colorado Springs like a stalker more times than would make anyone comfortable. That every time he got a little tipsy out with friends it was her number he wanted to drunk-text.

That he'd never stopped dreaming about her even when he'd forced his mind not to think of her while awake.

When he'd seen her holding that baby today, an icy panic had gripped his heart. Because she'd been in danger, but more because he'd thought he'd been too late to right his wrongs. She'd met someone else and fallen in love and made sweet beautiful babies.

When Brooke had stood up and taken the baby from Laura and he'd realized they weren't Laura's children, something had snapped into place for him. He hadn't realized it at that moment but he sure as hell realized it now.

He wasn't waiting any longer. He had to make

things right with Laura. He didn't know why he'd waited until now to start trying.

By her own admission Laura wasn't married or seeing anyone. Joe planned to change that. If he could convince her to forgive him. That was a huge if.

But he planned to try. Fate, in the form of two moronic bank robbers, had brought them back together. It gave him the perfect opening to ease back into her life, to apologize in every way he knew how. And think of a few new creative ways if needed.

That would be his pleasure.

And if he couldn't talk her into giving their relationship a try, he could at least prove himself a friend to her. To erase from his mind forever that haunted, shattered look that had taken over her features when he'd let the press and gossip columns get the best of him and convince him he could do better than Laura Birchwood.

News flash: he couldn't.

He wouldn't blame her if she would never become romantically involved with him again, but he was going to try to convince her.

Starting tonight. He'd take a note from his get-whatever-I-want past playbook and follow her home. He'd charm her into going out with him.

He began walking back toward the bank. As soon as he cleared the building he could feel eyes on him. Press and bystanders were all taking pictures and recording the scene and him. Most weren't looking at him, just knew something exciting had happened at the bank.

But a few people in the crowd knew who he was. He could feel eyes following him in particular. It never failed to make him a little uncomfortable when people seemed to be hostage "groupies."

Derek, Lillian and Jon were talking to the sheriff when Joe walked up to them.

"We'll get the rest of the statements and proceed from there. It looks like the manager and assistant manager of the bank were the only ones injured and neither of them seriously." Jon nodded at Joe in greeting.

That was good. Hopefully the judge would take that into consideration when sentencing Ricky and Bobby, aka Mitchell and Michael Goldman.

"Lillian, Joe and I are going to head back to Omega HQ since you seem to have everything under control," Derek said, shaking the sheriff's hand.

"I'm going to stay around for the rest of the evening, if that's okay," Jon told the sheriff. "I work crisis management in a lot of cases for Omega and may be able to help you with press or any questions you have."

"We appreciate Omega sending you so quickly." Sheriff Richardson turned to Joe. "And we especially appreciate what you did in there. That you kept it from becoming bloody."

Joe shook the man's outstretched hand. "The Goldman brothers didn't really want to harm anybody in my opinion. They just made some bad decisions, which led to panicking and more bad decisions."

"Either way, me and my men are thankful for how the situation got handled today. I'm sure the hostages are, too."

Jon and Sheriff Richardson turned back toward the bank while Lillian, Derek and Joe began walking the blocks to where the helicopter had been landed.

"Alright, mission completed. Let's get home," Derek said.

Lillian nodded as they began to make their way up to the roof. Joe wanted to move quicker, to rush them, so he could get back to HQ and back to Laura. But he knew it wouldn't accomplish anything but cause them to dig into why he was in such a hurry. Joe was rarely in a hurry.

But getting to Laura, seeing her again? Touching her again in any way she would allow…

His urgency continued to grow.

He wanted to give her as little time as possible to fortify walls against him. That was why he was going to see her tonight.

Derek rode in the copilot seat next to Lillian, leaving Joe in the back by himself. That was fine. He felt some of the pressure inside him start to loosen as the overhead blades began to whirl and they became airborne.

"Hey, did anyone get video footage of Matarazzo in just his undies?" Lillian asked. "I didn't have a great view from where I was in the elevator shaft."

"Oh, you better believe it, sister." Derek's amusement was obvious. "I wouldn't want anyone at Omega to miss that."

Joe didn't even care.

LAURA WALKED INTO her small house in Fountain, Colorado, just south of Colorado Springs, an hour and a half after leaving Joe standing by the side of the bank building.

What a day. She didn't know which shook her more, two idiots running around with guns or facing Joe again.

She was a liar; she knew which shook her more. But she had kept it together, talked to him reasonably, calmly, like an adult.

And then turned and ran away like a five-year-old.

Laura sighed. She could've handled the situation with more aplomb, more pride, more professionalism—all of which seemed to have evacuated her presence when Joe entered her personal space. Thank goodness that only happened every six years so far.

She changed out of her business suit of a black pencil skirt and blazer coupled with a white blouse and slipped on brown leggings and a chunky-knit, cream-colored sweater. She looked at herself in the mirror. The person she saw looking back at her didn't cause her to cringe or turn away. Laura knew who she was. Not gorgeous by any stretch of the imagination, but she was reasonably attractive—brown hair, hazel eyes, a nose just a touch too small, lips a touch too big. Her five-foot-four-inch frame was just average. As a matter of fact everything about her looks was just sort of average.

Nobody was going to stop and follow her down the streets whistling and catcalling because of her looks, but no one was ever going to run away screaming either.

It was only when you placed her against the backdrop of someone as gorgeous as, say, Joe Matarazzo, that anyone looked at Laura and used words like plain Jane, doleful, or *reverse beauty and the beast*.

All of those had been said about her when she'd dated Joe. Mostly by people in gossip blogs. Joe had told her to ignore all press, so she had. She thought he had, too. Until he'd proved otherwise by ending their relationship so suddenly.

That had hurt, mostly because the blow had been so unexpected.

When they'd first met she'd expected it. She'd worked nights waiting tables so she could go to law school during the day. He'd come in with a couple of buddies and flirted outrageously. She'd laughed him off, not taking him even the least bit seriously.

After all, how could someone who looked like Joe Matarazzo be interested in someone like her?

But he'd pursued her. Her twenty-three-year-old, slightly socially awkward self hadn't had a chance against Joe when he'd set his sights on her.

And she would admit, he didn't have to pursue her long. She gave in. When else would she get the opportunity to have a fling with someone like Joe? He'd been handsome and charming and popular, and the sparks had flown.

She'd been expecting the blow then, too. Once

he'd gotten what he'd wanted physically, she thought he'd be gone. But he'd stayed.

Laura knew she had her perks: she was focused and driven when it came to her career, but also cared about people. She tried to be honest and live by the golden rule. But she definitely wasn't someone who would be labeled as witty, or the life of the party, or a breathtaking beauty.

She didn't think she'd keep Joe's attention for long. But when weeks had turned into months and he was still always around, she'd started to believe their relationship was going somewhere.

She'd let her guard down. Let herself believe he was falling for her the way she was falling for him.

That had made the unexpected blow so much harder to take when it finally came. When he'd called off the relationship after they'd been together just over six months, with no warning at all.

Laura straightened as she focused on her reflection in the mirror, smoothing her sweater down. That was all in the past. No more thinking about Joe Matarazzo. Fate had dumped them together today, but that didn't mean anything.

The doorbell rang and Laura checked the clock. It must be little Brad next door. The seven-year-old sometimes came over to play video games on the weekends. His father was deployed in the military and his mom had her hands full with his three-year-old twin sisters.

Good. An hour's worth of Mario Kart would cure whatever ailed her.

She bounded down the stairs and swung by and opened the door, not stopping to look at Brad on her way to the kitchen. She needed some fortification if she was going to take on the neighbor boy. He was a fiend at the driving game.

"Brad, come on in. I'm going to throw a frozen pizza in the oven. It's all over for you tonight, kiddo. No amount of coins or stunt boosts are going to save you this time."

"I'm not sure what stunt boosts are, but I guess I better learn if they're needed to save me."

Not Brad's voice. Joe's voice. Laura dropped the pizza on the counter and walked back to her foyer.

"What are you doing here?"

"You don't sound as excited to see me as you did about seeing Brad." Joe's smile was charming, gorgeous. Laura had to force herself not to give in to the appeal, to keep her expression cool.

"That may be because the most hurtful thing Brad has ever done to me was launch a red koopa shell at my Mario Kart vehicle." She turned back toward the kitchen. "And even then he felt pretty bad about it."

"Laura…"

Turning her back to him had been a mistake. His long legs had closed the distance between them quickly and silently and now he was right behind her.

"What do you want, Joe?"

He touched her gently on the arm. It was totally unfair that she could still feel sparks of attraction where his skin touched hers. She didn't turn around.

"Seeing you today… I just wanted to say I'm sorry. I—"

"Apology accepted. You can go."

It hurt Laura to say the words. But it was better this way.

Joe was quiet for a long time before coming around to stand in front of her. "You have every right not to ever talk to me again. But let me just take you out one time. Let the person I've become in the last six years talk to the person you've become."

He reached down and grasped her hands; she could feel his thumbs stroking the back of her palms. "We're not the same people we were then,

Laura. I don't expect you to get involved with me, but I would appreciate it a great deal if you would just let me take you out one time to apologize for my stupidity then."

His clear blue eyes were sincere. His face pleading, engaging. A curl of sandy brown hair fell over his forehead as he gazed down at her, and hope lit his features. Laura couldn't resist him when he was like this. Nobody could resist him when he was like this.

Like you were the center of his world.

But she'd been here before. She couldn't forget that. This time she'd take some control. She thought about just cooking the pizza she'd gotten out and feeding them both that. Letting him say what he had to say. But being trapped inside a house with him where there was a bed, or a bathtub, or the couch or the kitchen floor nearby was probably not a good idea.

"Fine," she told him, her breath escaping her body when his worried look turned into one of joy, lighting up his eyes. "I'll go out with you. But no place fancy. No romance and candles. As a matter of fact, I'll pick the place."

His suppressed half smile only added to his charm. Damn him. "Yes, ma'am."

She poked him in his chest. "And you keep your hands to yourself. You got that?"

His smile turned downright wicked.

She was in trouble.

Chapter Five

Joe seemed different. An hour later, sitting in the restaurant where they'd first met when she'd been a waitress and he'd come in with his friends after a night of partying, she had to admit he wasn't the same man she'd known six years ago.

He'd grown up.

Although he was two years older, in their previous relationship Laura had always been the more mature one. Now Joe seemed more balanced, more focused. She had no doubt of the cause for that.

"So Omega Sector, huh?" She leaned back against the booth across from him, having finished her meal, and took a sip of her wine. "I never would've pegged you for law enforcement."

"I didn't have much education, but I had a pretty developed skill set. I decided to see if I could put that to use."

Laura raised her eyebrow. She definitely remembered certain skills Joe had, but was pretty sure that wasn't what he meant. She tugged at her sweater feeling a little overheated. "Oh yeah?"

"I had a very observant, honest friend who pointed out to me that I had more potential than to just be a trust fund baby. That I had skills in observation, listening, adaptability. That I was calm under pressure and that people genuinely seemed to like me."

Laura's eyes snapped to his face. *She* had said that to him. Had truly believed it. But she hadn't dreamed he would take her words and change his whole life.

"Wow," she whispered.

"Yeah, wow." He took a sip of his wine. "I re-paid the favor by saying some of the cruelest, most ridiculous words that have ever left my mouth. Ever left *anybody's* mouth."

"Joe..."

He reached over and grasped her hand. "I want to make sure you know I'm sorry. That a day has not gone by where I haven't regretted those words. I've nearly called you or come to your house dozens of times, but—"

"Joe." She stopped him, shaking her head. "You were right. About us. About me not being the right type of woman for you. You were right."

"No." The hand not holding hers hit the table just loud enough to cause her to jump. "I was not right. Whatever the opposite of right is, that's what I was."

Laura couldn't help but smile. "Wrong?"

Joe laughed and sat back, releasing her hand, the tension easing from his face. "Yeah, wrong. Wrong to let myself be convinced of it, wrong to say it, wrong not to have apologized for it before now."

Laura was not one to hold a grudge. She'd learned long ago that bitterness against him only hurt herself and had let it go.

"Well, I accept your apology and even appreciate it. What you said, what those gossip sites said, helped me turn a corner. I realized I was never going to be beautiful, but that I could at least make more of an effort. Style my hair, wear more makeup, make more attractive clothing choices."

Joe's jaw got tight as he studied her. "You look great now, but you were fine just like you were."

"I was…comfortable just like I was. But I realized when I started my own law firm how important a professional image was. Like it or not, studies show that attractiveness affects your level of trustworthiness and credibility with people. I needed to change my image."

His expression grew pained. "Laura—"

She smiled at him. She wasn't trying to make him feel bad—the opposite in fact. She wanted him to know that what had happened between them had helped her. "I'm just trying to say that I grew from the situation, like you did."

"But—"

"No more talk about the past. Okay? Or at least that part. We were young. We were stupid. Let's just agree and move on."

He looked like he was going to say something more but stopped and nodded.

Joe told her about some of the training he'd had to do to become an Omega Sector agent and some of his exploits since joining them. Laura told him about her law firm and how it had grown over the last year.

The words flowed easily. Lightly. This was how it had always been between the two of them: comfortable, relaxed. Only when other people had entered the equation had it gotten difficult and complicated.

Laura became aware of eyes on them partway through their conversation but tried to ignore it. Someone like Joe always had eyes on him. How could women not stare, even if they didn't know who he was? But Laura didn't like it. Didn't like the thoughts that began to enter her head. Were they wondering what Joe was doing with someone like her?

Amazing how the blackness could creep in unbidden. No one had said anything; maybe no one was even thinking anything, but Laura could already feel her confidence plummet. She picked at the food she'd ordered, no longer able to enjoy the meal.

She couldn't do this again.

She wasn't mad at Joe, the opposite, in fact. Spending time with him just made her remember why she had fallen for him six years ago.

Which was also adding to her panic.

She'd been around him a little over an hour and she was already back to the person she'd been. Worried about her looks, about what people thought. How many different ways did she have to be told that she and Joe were from two different realms before she accepted it as the truth?

Somebody clicked their picture. The flash made Laura wince.

Joe turned calmly to the man. "Hi, we're having dinner if you don't mind." His voice was friendly but firm. Laura saw the manager heading toward their table to ward off any problems, but the man with the camera left.

It could've just been anyone who recognized Joe and wanted to snap his picture.

It could've been someone from a major gossip rag.

Either way Laura knew she couldn't stay. She put her napkin down beside her plate; she felt like she had a knot in her stomach that wouldn't ease. Joe studied her with concern.

"I'm sorry, but I can't do this. I can't be here

with you, can't do this again. Thank you for dinner, thank you for the apology. I wish you the best, Joe."

She started to stand, but he grasped her hand before she could.

"Laura, you're panicking. Don't. Please." She felt his thumb brush over the back of her palm. "It was just a photograph and doesn't mean anything."

"No, what it was was a reminder. You are you and I am me. Our worlds aren't compatible. You would've thought I learned that lesson well six years ago."

"It doesn't have to be that way. I wasn't prepared tonight, but I can take measures to protect you from the press. From the gossip."

She tilted her head to the side. "Who's going to protect me against you, Joe?"

He gripped her hand more firmly. "I don't want you to protect yourself from me. You don't need to, because I'm not going to do anything that will cause you harm. I give you my word."

Laura shook her head. She believed that he meant it, but that didn't change anything. "I can't be the person who opened up to you so completely before. That person got crushed in the fray. I don't think she exists anymore."

"Then open up the woman who does exist." A moment of pain crossed his features. "I'm sorry. I know I hurt you badly. I wish I could take it all back."

Laura let out a sigh. "I'm not trying to make you feel bad, truly. It's just I don't know if I can open up to you. If I even want to." Didn't know if the price would be too high. "All I know right now is that it's been a long day. I need some space. Some time."

Joe stared at her for long moments. She knew he wanted to say more, wanted to plead his case. Part of her wanted him to, but she knew it could just lead to disaster.

He nodded and let go of her hand, leaning back in his seat. "Okay, you're right. I'm trying to rush this. To force it. And that's not what I meant to do at all. So we'll take it slow."

"Joe…" She wanted to tell him to just leave her alone for good, that she didn't want him around her, but couldn't do it. She couldn't force herself to say the words.

Because she knew they would be a lie.

He leaned forward pinning her with his blue eyes. "I'm not giving up, Laura. I'll let you go now, but I want you to know I'm not giving up."

LAURA THOUGHT ABOUT his words the entire way home, thankful she'd had the foresight to insist they drive separate cars to the restaurant. She thought about the intensity of his blue eyes and the way his entire body had leaned toward her as he told her he wasn't giving up.

She had no doubt he meant what he said.

But despite the attraction fairly simmering in

her blood for him, Laura knew she couldn't go through it again. Joe Matarazzo might be the most handsome, charming, wealthy man she'd ever met, but he was no good for her.

She would have to make him understand. Make him see that she wasn't just playing hard-to-get. That her very survival depended on him choosing to leave her, and the life she'd built, alone.

But was that really what she wanted? Deep down did she hope for something different? For him to pursue her again as he once had?

She had pushed those types of thoughts immediately out of her head for so long that she could no longer even answer them honestly. Even to herself.

She wished the universe would send her some sort of sign.

It did, with a vengeance.

One moment she was driving down a relatively deserted patch of Highway 87, the next another car had slammed into the back driver's side of Laura's vehicle.

She screamed as her head struck the side window and struggled to hold on to consciousness, her vision immediately blurry. Her car flew out of control, spinning in a sideways direction almost off the road. She jerked the steering wheel but it didn't seem to do any good. She looked over her shoulder and found the vehicle that had hit her still pushed up against her Toyota.

Was the other car trying to ram her toward the safety rail on the side of the road?

Laura glanced in that direction for just a second. She knew this part of Highway 87 pretty well. The drop past that safety rail was steep. She would definitely flip if she went over the edge.

Looking back again at the car still locked against hers, Laura slammed on the brakes with both feet, causing her car to stop and the other one to separate from it and speed past. Once her car wasn't trapped by the other, Laura had control of the steering again and overcorrected, causing her to swing around backward and land hard up against the rail. Her head flew back the other way from the force of the hit.

Her breath sawed in and out of her chest. That driver had to be drunk. Idiot had almost killed them both.

In the rearview mirror Laura noticed the other driver tap the brakes and wondered if the close call with death had sobered the person up enough to realize what they had done. But the car sped farther away. Laura tried to get a glimpse of the license plate but her vision was too blurry.

She sat for long minutes trying to take inventory of herself. Nothing seemed to be broken. She definitely had a knot on her head where she'd cracked it against the window and her hands were shaking. But it all seemed to be pretty minor bumps and bruises, considering she'd almost been run off the road. Overall, she considered herself lucky.

An older couple pulled up behind her—well, in front of her since her car was facing backward—and immediately got out to help. They opened the passenger side door and assisted her across the front seats and out of the car. The police were called and at the scene soon enough.

Laura was tempted to call Joe. He would still be nearby and she knew he would come immediately.

She also knew there was no way he wasn't going to end up in her bed if she did that.

She would attend to her bumps and bruises herself. At least right now they were just on her body; if she called Joe she was sure he'd soothe all her physical aches. But the ones he'd leave on her heart wouldn't be so easily healed.

Chapter Six

Convincing Laura to let him back into her life wasn't going to be as easy as Joe had hoped. Not that he had really expected it was going to be easy. As a matter of fact, he would've sworn before Friday there was no way in hell she was ever going to let him back into her life. That she would punch him if he ever dared show his face around her again.

Although he had known she was a better person than that. She had even accepted his apology. But he knew when she left the restaurant she had no intention of ever seeing him again. The person who had snapped their picture had spooked her. Maybe she could agree that Joe wouldn't be cruel, wouldn't say unkind things to or about her, but the press?

Joe tended to be the press's darling, but he knew they could often be harsh and callous. They certainly had been to Laura.

What Joe said to her when they broke up had been unkind, but what the gossip sites had published about her while they had dated had been downright brutal.

Once he and Laura had been seen together multiple times over a few weeks, one blog had gone so far as to print a picture of her and point out her top ten flaws. Publicly and without mercy. He hoped she had never seen that, but wouldn't have been surprised if she had.

Joe had been stupid enough to begin to believe some of what was printed. The digs against her that pointed out her flaws. He would never be so idiotic as to pay any attention to gossip sites now—particularly since he knew how much those sites got wrong—but had let it get the better of him then. Let the sites, and some stupid friends who had his ear, convince him that Laura just wasn't the right one for him.

Because it was much easier to dwell on that than to face the real scenario: he'd been falling for Laura.

Complete and utter panic because he had been falling so hard and so quickly for her. She'd been real, so full of life, and honest and passionate about helping people. She'd had a smile that lit up an entire room.

She still did. Still was. All of those things.

Had he really ever thought Laura unattractive six years ago?

No, never. No matter what the gossip sites had said about her physical appearance, Joe had always found himself overwhelmingly attracted to her. The passion between them had sizzled. Looking at other women had been unappealing.

And honestly, another reason why he'd panicked. Because for the first time he was in a relationship where he wasn't thinking about who his next conquest would be. Wasn't feeling trapped or penned in, when he knew he should be.

He was too young for love. So when his friends and random websites who didn't give a damn about Joe or his happiness had told him Laura wasn't good enough, he'd latched onto that idea.

He shook his head now at the idiot he'd been then.

Getting back into Laura's life wasn't going to be easy, not that he blamed her one bit. But like he'd told her Friday at the restaurant: he wasn't giving up.

He'd sent flowers Saturday, stargazer lilies, her favorite. On Sunday he'd had four pints of Ben & Jerry's ice cream delivered to her house, picking out the ones he remembered she'd always loved when they'd sat on her couch watching football games together.

He didn't expect either of these gestures to

make a difference; Laura would see straight through them. But they were a start.

It was Monday morning now and he was walking into the room that held his desk at Omega, an open area where most of the Critical Response Division team members' desks were arranged. The team wasn't at them a lot, but it was the home base. The floor-to-ceiling windows of the room provided a gorgeous view of the Rocky Mountains to the west.

At least they normally did. Today they were covered—completely, top to bottom—with photocopied images of Joe in his well-fitting, black boxer briefs. Hundreds of them, all different shots from the scene at the bank when he'd been proving to Ricky and Bobby he was unarmed.

And—*oh joy*—they all had comments. Most of them read something asinine like "he's unarmed but his weapon works just fine."

The audible snickers from the nearby desks

surrounded Joe as he walked over to the pictures, studying all the different shots.

He knew everyone was waiting to see if he was going to get angry or embarrassed. He wasn't.

He took one down and turned to face his colleagues. "Hey, I'm going to use these to re-cover my bathroom if that's okay with everyone. Most gorgeous wallpaper I've ever seen."

The laughs burst out then.

"Yeah, you guys are a riot." But he smiled, beginning to take the sheets down. "I should leave these up here. It would serve you all right."

Lillian, along with Ashton Fitzgerald, another SWAT member, jumped up to help him. "It was just such a memorable occasion." Lillian smiled at him. "We wanted to make sure everyone at Omega had the pleasure of experiencing it."

Steve Drackett, head of the Critical Response Division, walked out of his office and looked around. He rolled his eyes. "I don't even want to know what this is all about. I need SWAT members in my office. We've got a situation."

Ashton, Lillian and a few others turned to follow Steve. "By the way, Joe, nice skivvies." Steve winked at him.

Joe watched as they left, glad, not for the first time, that he wasn't a part of the SWAT team. Let them go shoot all the bad people. Joe had to write up the report from Friday anyway.

He hadn't gotten very far in the paperwork when his phone chirped with an incoming email.

Sarah Conner, an old girlfriend.

Wow, that was a blast from the past. He and Sarah had dated briefly not quite a year ago. Nothing serious, just a few weeks of a good time. She hadn't expected anything from him nor had he expected anything from her. She'd ended it because she desired to have someone around more often and Joe couldn't be since he traveled so much for his job. Everything had been on good terms although they hadn't really spoken since.

He opened the email, not sure exactly what he was expecting. Maybe her telling him that she'd found someone and planned to get married. Instead, the email contained a brief, cryptic message.

I need to talk to you. It's important. Come to my place ASAP.

Joe wasn't sure what to do with the email. On one hand he wasn't at all interested in seeing Sarah, not romantically at least. But it sounded like maybe she needed some sort of help.

He called Sarah's number but didn't get an answer. He'd been to her place enough times to know where it was in south Colorado Springs.

Not quite as far south as Fountain, where Laura lived, but definitely in that general direction. He would go to Sarah's house, then after he took care of whatever she needed, he would stop by and say hello to Laura in person.

Maybe offer her one of his colleagues' pieces of art. She'd love that. He could use it to prove he didn't take himself so seriously anymore.

That would probably go further than flowers or ice cream.

Regardless he'd be able to see Laura. Even if it was only for a few minutes, he'd take it.

Joe let one of Steve Drackett's secretaries— all beautiful, intelligent women—know that he was going out to deal with some residual issues with Friday's case and would be back later in the afternoon. They knew how to contact him if there was a hostage situation for which he was needed. But it sounded like SWAT was going to be busy somewhere else.

Joe's Jaguar F-TYPE sports car made short work of the miles to Sarah's house. Although he was curious about what Sarah had to say, he was anxious to see Laura.

He pulled up to Sarah's house, a nice chalet-style place off on its own. It didn't look like anyone was home, which only made Joe happier. But he'd driven all the way here; he might as well at least try to see what Sarah wanted.

Joe parked and bounded up to the steps leading to Sarah's front door. He rang the doorbell and waited. Nothing. He rang it again, but received no response.

Well, he could at least tell Sarah he tried.

He knocked just in case the doorbell wasn't working and was surprised when the door pushed open under his knuckles. It hadn't been completely closed.

He knocked again, still staying outside, but stuck his head in slightly and called out.

"Sarah, you around? It's Joe."

Nothing.

Something wasn't right here. Joe took the slightest step inside.

"Hey, Sarah? You emailed me to come over. I just wanted to see what's going on."

Still no answer.

Joe went back to his car and got his Glock from the glove compartment. Although he didn't use it often, it was still his official Omega weapon. He was licensed to use it. Trained to use it.

He prayed he didn't need to use it now.

He ran back to the door. "Sarah, I'm coming inside. I'm armed. Let me know if you're in there so no one gets hurt."

Still nothing. Joe went from being afraid he might be walking in on Sarah in the shower to hoping it. Embarrassing, but at least she would be alive to be embarrassed.

He checked all the ground floor rooms first. When he found nothing in the kitchen or living room he slowly made his way upstairs.

He saw her immediately when he entered the master bedroom. Sarah laid sprawled facedown on the bed, naked, arm over her face as if she was sleeping off a hangover.

Except for the blood that had pooled all around her.

He rushed over to check for her pulse, just in case, but knew as soon as he felt the coolness of her skin that she was definitely dead, probably had been for hours.

Joe took a few deep breaths to center himself, focus on what had happened. He was an Omega agent, had seen dead bodies before, but never someone he'd known so personally.

Training took over. This was now a crime scene, and that definitely wasn't Joe's area of expertise. He needed to call in the specialists. Both local law enforcement and Omega.

He speed-dialed Steve Drackett's direct number.

"Joe, what's going on?" Steve said in way of greeting. Joe didn't call his direct line very often and only when there was a problem.

But there'd never been one like this before.

"Steve, I've got an issue. Dead woman, an ex-girlfriend of mine. I got a message from her earlier asking me to come by but when I got here she was dead. Murdered."

"You sure it was a murder?"

"Unmistakable."

He heard Steve's muttered expletive. "Okay, call the locals and get them there. I'll send Brandon and Andrea to see if they pick up on anything the locals might miss."

Brandon Han was the most brilliant profiler Omega had. Joe knew both him and Andrea Gordon, a talented behavioral analyst who was now Brandon's partner on most cases. Having them here would help, or at the very least help Joe's peace of mind.

"Thanks, Steve."

"Don't touch anything, okay? You should probably walk back out the way you came and wait for the locals outside."

Joe nodded, still looking at Sarah, then real-ized his boss couldn't see him. "Yeah, okay."

Steve sighed. "I'm sorry, Joe. It's always hard when it's someone you know. Even an ex."

Joe said his goodbyes and then called 911, re-porting the death. Then he stood staring at Sarah for a long time.

He hadn't really felt much for the woman, be-sides a physical attraction. He wished he knew more about her, who he should call, family or whatever, but he didn't. The police would have to handle that.

Who would've wanted to kill Sarah? She was an accountant, or in public relations or some-thing like that. Not a job that tended to develop enemies.

Had she known about the danger? Is that why she had emailed Joe? The cryptic message she'd sent didn't provide many clues.

Finally he did what Steve had suggested and moved outside to wait for the locals. He would need to identify himself as law enforcement and let them know why he was here. Otherwise an armed man at a murder scene tended to make cops pretty nervous.

Joe stood leaning against his car, still trying to wrap his head around this entire situation, when the locals came speeding in, sirens blaring. Four separate squad cars and an ambulance. Must be a slow day around town.

Joe had his Omega credentials out in his hand, extended so the officers could see that he clearly did not mean them any harm. The men stopped to talk to him and he explained the situation, gave them Sarah's info, then waited as three of them rushed in. The other two stayed with Joe, hands noticeably near their sidearms.

When the three men exited Sarah's house they were moving much less quickly. There was no hurry; nothing could be done to help her now. The officer in charge nodded at the two men who'd been tasked with babysitting Joe while the others were inside.

"Is the coroner on his way?"

"Yeah."

"Okay, let's rope this area off. Neighbors are going to start wondering what's going on."

The man in charge turned to Joe. "I'm Detective Jack Thompson. So you work for Omega Sector. Were you here on official business? Something to do with a case?"

"No. I used to date the victim, about a year ago. She emailed me this morning, asked me to come by."

One of Thompson's eyebrows lifted suspiciously. "Is that so? Did things end badly between you two when you broke up?"

"No, we were never very serious. Neither of us was upset when we decided it wasn't working out."

"I see." Officer Thompson jotted a couple sentences down in his notebook. "And did you and

Ms. Conner talk to each other much since the breakup?"

"No, maybe once or twice, but not really that I remember."

"But she just happened to email you this morning and asked you to come by?" Disbelief clearly tinted the man's tone.

Joe didn't take offense to the question. He could admit it was a little weird that he hadn't spoken with Sarah for months then the day she contacted him, she winded up dead.

"Yes."

Thompson studied Joe's car for a moment before turning back to Joe. The nice vehicle obviously wasn't winning Joe any points with the detective. "What exactly do you do for Omega Sector, Mr. Matarazzo?"

"Joe is one of the finest hostage negotiators we have." The sentence came from behind him. Joe turned to find Brandon Han and Andrea Gordon.

Brandon showed his credentials to Officer

Thompson. "We'll need to get inside, if that's possible."

Thompson's lips pursed and his eyes narrowed at Joe. "Fine. But I'm going in to supervise, make sure everything is handled correctly. Please stick around Agent Matarazzo, in case we have any more questions." He left to enter the house.

"Sorry about your friend, Joe," Andrea said, touching him on the arm.

"Thanks," he told the striking blonde. "And thanks for coming, you guys."

Brandon shook his hand. "No problem. We're going to go inside, see if we spot anything the locals might miss. Will you be okay out here?"

"Yeah, I'm fine. You guys do whatever you need to do to help with the case." He watched as Brandon led Andrea toward the front door, a protective hand on the small of her back.

Joe leaned back against his car and got comfortable. This was going to take most of the day;

Officer Thompson had just started with his questions, and didn't seem interested in making this easy or comfortable for him. Joe wasn't going to be able to see Laura as he'd hoped. That was probably for the best; he didn't want to drag her into this anyway.

Chapter Seven

By Wednesday afternoon Laura was cursing Joe Matarazzo's name. Damn the man. Damn him because for just a split second she thought he had really changed. That he wasn't the selfish playboy he once had been.

After the accident on Friday, her aches had made her want to forget all about Joe. But then the flowers—or more importantly the fact that he'd remembered her favorite type of flowers were stargazer lilies—had caused her to think maybe Joe really had changed. Then Sunday the ice cream had arrived.

She had to admit the frozen stuff—again, all

her favorite flavors—had melted her heart a little bit. Brought back memories of their time together.

She had fully expected him to show up or call on Monday. When he hadn't, she'd been okay with it, and even wondered if she should call him and tell him thanks, but decided not to. When she didn't hear from Joe all day Tuesday, she'd gotten a little miffed.

By Wednesday at lunch, Laura was disgusted with herself and Joe. If he didn't want to see her again, that was fine. But he shouldn't act like he wanted to then not follow through.

And her? How many times was she going to fall for his sexy-boy appeal and wit?

There was nothing more dangerous than a man with charm. And Joe Matarazzo had it in spades.

And Laura was just an idiot to keep trusting his not-really promises. *I'm not giving up.* It had at least been true for two days.

So she could admit she was a little short-tempered when her law office phone rang at 4:00 p.m. Her assistant was gone for the day so Laura answered the phone herself, unable to keep her irritation out of her voice.

"Law Offices of Coach, Birchwood and Winchley."

"Wow, do you always answer the phone like you're considering strangling the entire neighborhood?"

Joe. It figured that he would know she was about to write him off for good and call now. The man's timing was impeccable.

"No, I'm just considering strangling one person."

That quieted him.

"I'm sorry I haven't been able to get in touch before now," he finally said. "Things have been complicated."

"Things tend to always be complicated with you, Joe."

He gave a short bark of laughter, but there

didn't seem to be very much humor in it. "Well, believe it or not, I'm about to make things more complicated."

Laura rolled her eyes. "Why don't I just save you the trouble and stop you right there. I've been thinking over the last couple of days and realize I need to stand firm on what I told you at the restaurant on Friday. You and I are better off away from each other."

"Laura—"

"This isn't about the not calling." Damn it, why had she said that? Now it sounded like she was pissy because he hadn't called. Which, of course, she was. "I just think you and I should leave the past where it was."

"Laura—"

She didn't want to hear what he had to say, knowing if he gave her an excuse, she'd believe him. "Joe, I just can't go through the back-and-forth and you changing your mind."

"Laura, *stop*." She'd never heard that particular air of forcefulness in his tone. Joe tended to always be so laid-back most people forgot how strong he could be when needed. It was enough to stop her midthought. "I am willing to discuss this all with you at a later time, because there's no way I'm going to let you run away from us. But I'm not calling about that."

"Then what are you calling about?"

"Have you had a chance to watch the news or get online to read the news over the last couple of days?"

No. She'd been forcing herself to stay too busy to even allow herself to do anything as stupid as Google Joe Matarazzo. "I haven't, sorry. I've been too busy at work. Why?"

"I'm calling because I need you as a lawyer. A woman I used to know was murdered on Monday."

And now didn't she feel like an ass? "Oh my gosh, Joe, that's terrible. But you shouldn't need a lawyer just because someone you knew was murdered. Unless they caught you in the act."

"It wasn't quite that bad, but it wasn't good either."

Okay, that didn't sound promising. "Still—"

"And then it happened again this morning."

"What?"

"Another one of my ex-girlfriends was killed this morning."

As far as excuses went for not calling, two dead ex-girlfriends in two and a half days was a pretty good one. Laura heard noise in the background.

"Joe, where are you right now? Were you arrested?"

"They haven't brought any formal charges against me, but they're holding me for questioning. I'm at the Colorado Springs downtown station."

Laura had already grabbed her purse and

blazer. "Don't say anything to anyone. I'll be right there."

"Laura, there's more. Both women contacted me just before they died. And I found both bodies."

That really didn't look good. "I'm coming, Joe. Just don't answer any questions until I get there. Okay?"

"Don't you need to ask me if I did it?"

"No. Just don't talk to anyone." Laura hung up the phone and rushed out of her office.

She didn't need to ask if Joe was guilty; she knew he wasn't. Joe might be a lot of things Laura didn't like, but he wasn't a killer.

IF JOE HAD been the police, he would've brought himself in for questioning too.

When he'd received a message this morning from Jessica Johannsen, another one of his ex-girlfriends, asking him to come to her town house in the north part of Colorado Springs, Joe hadn't thought anything bad about it. He figured she'd just heard about Sarah's death, read a newspaper or saw a news report, and wanted to talk to him. To make this about her instead of Sarah.

Jessica had always been sort of clingy, not someone capable of handling much emotional stress. And she loved drama. Joe had never really been interested in her, although that hadn't stopped him from dating her for a few weeks about two years ago.

Jessica had had delicate features with long black hair and icy blue eyes. The press had delighted at what a lovely pair they'd made.

She'd bored him silly.

But he hadn't been surprised to receive a message from her after Sarah's death. Jessica would want to be held, patted, to be the center of attention even though Sarah's death had nothing to do with her.

She'd asked him to meet her this morning in

her text message. He'd texted her back and told her he was busy.

He hadn't wanted to take the time to see Jessica. He'd wanted to see Laura. After Monday's incident with Sarah, he hadn't been able to call or go see her as he'd planned. He'd spent all day on Tuesday cleaning up from Sarah's death: he'd talked to her parents since he'd been the one who'd found her body, he'd worked with Brandon and Andrea to see if they could gather any leads in figuring out who the killer might be.

He hadn't wanted to drag Laura into this whole sordid mess, so he hadn't contacted her at all.

But by Wednesday, all he'd wanted to do was see Laura. To just breathe in her smile and banter with her. It didn't need to be sexual; he just wanted to be with her.

So Jessica's text asking him to meet had just irritated Joe. When he told her no, and Jessica had sent another message telling him how scared she was, he'd decided to go see her. She'd just keep bugging him until he did.

As soon as Jessica's door floated open like Sarah's, Joe should've known there was a problem. He should've stopped right then, backed out and called the local police.

But he hadn't. Instead, just like with Sarah, he'd rushed inside to see what was going on because he didn't want to be there in the first place. He just wanted to talk to Jessica and leave.

He'd honestly thought Jessica would step out in some sort of outrageous negligee at any moment. Or even be completely naked wanting to seduce him. To get him to hold her while she cried fake tears about something that had nothing to do with her.

Jessica had been naked. But she'd been dead. Stabbed, just like Sarah.

All the lousy things he'd thought about her had rattled in his head as guilt swamped him. No one would ever hold Jessica Johannsen again as she cried fake or real tears.

Joe had called the locals immediately. He'd thought about calling Omega, too, but had stopped. Steve had helped him once but that's when it was just a random murder that happened to be Joe's ex.

Joe had no idea what it meant now that two of his exes were dead. But it wasn't a problem he was going to drag the Omega team into. He'd have to deal with this on his own.

Detective Thompson and the other local Colorado Springs police hadn't been nearly as friendly this time, not that Thompson had liked Joe much on Monday. They hadn't hauled him off in cuffs, but Thompson had left someone with Joe at the scene to watch him every minute. And once they were done with the crime scene, they'd asked to escort him to the station.

Escort, as in have him ride in the back of their squad car.

Then he'd sat in the interrogation room for two hours. He wasn't sure if they were trying to intimidate him, didn't know what to do with him, or what.

All he knew was that this looked bad. Really, really bad.

They hadn't arrested him, which was good. They did read him his rights, which was bad. They hadn't taken his phone—although that probably only happened if he was officially arrested—so he'd used his cell to call Laura. They hadn't told him he couldn't use it, so he'd figured he would. He had no idea how long he would be sitting in this room by himself, although he was sure someone was watching him, waiting to see what he would do.

Joe could've had a team of lawyers here, and would have if Laura had refused, but he wanted *her*. Other lawyers may be more vicious, more predatory in their methods of keeping their clients out of jail, but Laura believed in him.

Had always believed in him, even if she hadn't liked him.

And with all her intensity and intelligence he had no doubt she was a damn fine lawyer.

Detective Thompson entered the room. "Sorry to have kept you waiting, Matarazzo."

Joe highly doubted it.

"I heard you made a call. Got a lawyer."

Joe sat back. "It's my understanding that I'm allowed to have a lawyer if I'm being charged with something."

Thompson mirrored Joe's gesture, head tilting away, mouth downturned. "And it's my general experience that only people who are guilty need a lawyer. Besides, we haven't charged you with anything. You're free to go at any time."

Joe just wanted this to be over with. "I didn't kill Jessica Johannsen or Sarah Conner. I haven't had any contact with either of them for months."

"Interesting isn't it, though, that both women

just happened to contact you right before they died?"

What could Joe say to that?

He shrugged. "*Interesting* isn't the word I would use, but yes, it's strange."

"And you happened to find both bodies. Another interesting factor."

"I'm law enforcement, Thompson. One of the good guys."

Thompson moved in closer, leaning his elbows on the table that sat between them. "I know you're law enforcement, Joe. Is it okay if I call you Joe?" Thompson didn't wait for an answer. "You're part of Omega Sector, one of the top law enforcement agencies in the country."

"That's right."

"How does a guy like you end up working for Omega?"

"What do you mean, 'a guy like me'?"

"You don't need a job, right? You've got plenty

of money. So working for Omega as a negotiator is more like a hobby for you."

Joe pursed his lips. No, it wasn't a hobby for
him. But he could admit, most of the people in
the Critical Response Division probably thought
of him that way.

Seeing Joe's face, Thompson continued. "I'm
just saying, you're on the Omega roster, but
you're not really a member of the team, are you?
I don't notice any of them beating down the door
to get you out of here."

Joe forced himself not to show any emotion.
"I thought I wasn't under arrest, so why would
there be a need for them to come get me out?"

But Thompson's remark had hit home. Joe
wasn't part of the team at Omega. He got along
well with everyone, joked with them, did his job.
But none of them would call him a true member of the team.

The other man smirked. "Okay, I'll just take
you at your word that they'll be here if you're ar-

rested." But he obviously didn't believe that was true. "So you're a part of Omega. There's a lot of stress in law enforcement. Has been known to make strong men snap. Do something stupid. Add that stress to trying to balance two women and it could get a little crazy."

"I wasn't dating either of those women. And I definitely wasn't dating both of them." Joe shook his head.

"C'mon, Joe. I see some of the gossip sites. Dating more than one woman at a time is definitely not out of your realm of possibility."

"Barking up the wrong tree, Thompson."

"Alright, so you weren't dating them both. I can buy that. But did date them separately at one time. Maybe they got together and decided that you owed them something. A man could be forgiven for a lot of things when women decide to start blackmailing him. Especially someone who has as much as you do."

Joe had talked through enough hostage situations to recognize what was happening here. Thompson was trying to lull him into a false sense of security.

Joe hoped he wasn't this bad when he was doing his job. Because Thompson's contempt for him was just one step below obvious.

Joe gritted his teeth. "No. As far as I know, both Sarah and Jessica were wealthy in their own right, or at least they were last time I saw either of them."

"There's wealthy and then there's *Matarazzo* wealthy. I'm sure they don't have as much money as you do, and felt like maybe they deserved some of your wealth."

"If they did, they never mentioned it to me or implied it in any way."

"Women can just get it in their heads, you know, that a man owes them something, even when a guy doesn't make any promises. Them working together to try to bring you down, that would have to make you angry."

Joe was beginning to genuinely not like this guy. "Neither Jessica nor Sarah had anything against me. They weren't working together to blackmail me, or anything else as far as I know. They didn't even run in the same circles so I can't imagine they even knew each other."

"You're right. The only thing that links Sarah Conner and Jessica Johannsen to each other is their relationship with you." The detective sat back and stared.

Joe realized that had been Thompson's point the whole time. And Joe had walked him right to it. He should've listened to Laura when she said not to answer any questions.

"Why don't you give me a rundown on where you were on both Sunday and Tuesday nights between 3:00 and 6:00 a.m.?" Thompson asked.

He'd been completely alone. No one would be able to validate his whereabouts. Now he knew he definitely should've listened to Laura.

But damn it, he didn't kill those women. He had nothing to hide.

But the police clearly thought otherwise.

The door to the room opened. "My client won't be answering that, or any other questions, Detective Thompson. Either charge him or he's leaving."

Chapter Eight

"I need to go talk to my boss at Omega Sector." Joe gave Laura the address and she entered it into the GPS system on her phone.

He looked out the window while she drove, tension evident in his jaw and posture. Laura had never seen him so shaken. He tried to play it off, make it seem like it didn't really matter, but obviously it did.

He wasn't inhuman; two women he had known—intimately, no doubt—were dead. Just because he hadn't killed them didn't mean he didn't grieve.

Knowing he was the only link between the two women just added stress.

"What would you have answered Detective Thompson about your whereabouts?" she asked Joe as she took the interstate exit toward Omega Sector's headquarters in the northern section of Colorado Springs.

He shrugged. "I was home alone. Both nights. No alibi."

"That probably would have gotten you arrested, you know. That's why I told you not to answer any questions."

Joe turned to study her. "I didn't do it. That's why I thought I was safe answering questions."

"Yeah, well, the legal system doesn't always work that way. Especially when there are two dead young women and law enforcement is probably getting pressure to make an arrest."

"Not to mention the lead detective having a personal dislike and possible vendetta for me," Joe murmured. He shrugged. "Doesn't matter.

I didn't do it. And if they had arrested me there would still be a killer out on the loose."

"Let's give the cops a chance to do their job. They'll find something that clears you, I'm sure."

She hoped so.

It wasn't long before they pulled up to the large office complex that housed Omega Sector's Critical Response Division. It was a pretty unassuming set of buildings on the outside. She noticed construction was in process on another section of the complex.

"You guys expanding?"

"No, the forensic lab is being replaced after an explosion a few months ago."

"Oh my gosh. An accident?"

"No, deliberate. The people responsible for the Chicago bombing last May were trying to get rid of some evidence we had held there."

It suddenly hit home just exactly how dangerous Joe's job was. Somehow she hadn't thought of that last Friday when she saw him in action.

He'd talked to Ricky and Bobby like she'd seen him talk to dozens of other people: as though they were long-lost buddies and Joe had nothing in the world better to do than chat with them.

But he'd put his life on the line. Did that all the time. And all the money in the world wouldn't save him if some crazy hostage-taker just decided to shoot him.

She pulled into the parking garage where Joe directed her.

"Do you want to come inside with me?"

"Do you want me to?"

"Sure. Nothing is going to be said you aren't already aware of anyway."

They got out of the car and he led her through the main entrance where a security team checked her in. They walked through a maze of offices, most of them empty since it was nearly seven o'clock.

Joe pushed the door open to a room with four desks. Three were empty but at the fourth sat one of the most gorgeous women Laura had ever seen. Long, auburn hair with creamy smooth skin. Her posture impeccable in the black dress that seemed to both fit her like a second skin and be perfectly professional at the same time.

"Hey, Joe." She smiled at him, lips with a red gloss that looked as if it had just been applied moments before, revealing, of course, perfectly straight teeth. She stood up and walked over— in three-inch heels—to hug him. "I heard about your friends. I'm so sorry."

Joe hugged her back. Of course he would hug her back. What man in his right mind would not hug this woman back?

Laura stood there feeling more frumpy and dumpy by the nanosecond.

…Not the caliber of woman…

"Thanks, Cynthia." The detached and perfect Cynthia moved back to her desk. "I need to talk to Steve. I know he's still here since, well, he's always here. You're working late tonight."

She shrugged one delicate shoulder. "I'll let him know you're here. And…" She gestured toward Laura.

"Laura Birchwood. Lawyer and friend," Joe said.

Cynthia turned her smile on Laura. "Nice to meet you."

Laura did her best to smile back naturally although it probably came out looking more like a wounded animal in the throes of death. "Thanks."

Cynthia spoke on the phone for just a moment before standing and opening the door to her boss's inner office, leading them inside.

"Let me know if you need anything, Joe." Perfect smile again. Laura managed not to ask how she managed to look so perfect after working so late, especially in those heels. She glanced down at her own functionally comfortable flats.

The man behind the desk stood up and came around to shake Joe's hand. "I heard about the second victim. I'm sorry. I was worried when you didn't come in today."

"I've been a guest of the Colorado Springs PD for most of the day. This is Laura Birchwood, my friend and, as of earlier today, my lawyer."

"Steve Drackett." Laura shook the man's hand. He was older than Joe by at least a decade, but the slight blend of silver around his temples did nothing to detract from his handsomeness.

Was everyone who worked here gorgeous? At least it wasn't just the women.

Steve turned to Joe. "I'm sure Ms. Birchwood is an excellent attorney, but I would've sent Brandon Han in if you'd just called."

Joe shrugged, leading her to a seat and taking the one next to her as Steve went back behind his desk. "I didn't want to take up Omega resources for something that's personal. Plus, like you said, Laura is an excellent lawyer."

Steve looked at Joe for a long moment. "Is

it okay if you and I talk for a few minutes privately?"

"If it's about Sarah's and Jessica's deaths, then just go ahead and say it in front of Laura. I don't have any secrets from her."

"Colorado Springs PD of course called asking about you and your record here."

Laura nodded. She wasn't surprised.

"I want to help out with the investigation, Joe," Steve continued. "We have resources and personnel they don't have."

"Thanks, Steve."

Steve grimaced. "Don't thank me too soon. I think it's better if you take a leave of absence while the investigation takes place. That way no one can accuse anyone here of favoritism."

If Laura hadn't been looking right at Joe she would've missed it. The tiny crack under his easy smile.

Steve's request had hurt him.

But Joe certainly didn't show it to Steve. "Yeah, sure. I understand."

The older man looked like he felt bad. "I'm sorry, Joe. And I know you just donate your salary here to charity, but I'll have to suspend that, too. Officially you can't have anything to do with Omega while you're being investigated."

Joe stood, easy smile firmly in place, even the slightest crack Laura had noticed now gone. "I totally understand. You've got to do what's right for everyone overall."

"This will blow over in a week or two. They'll catch the real killer and everything will be back to normal. You'll be back in your rightful place here."

"Sure. Absolutely."

Steve grimaced again. "But right now I'll just have to ask you for your badge and sidearm."

LAURA TOOK JOE back to her house.

She wouldn't have done it if he had asked her

to. Or tried to put a move on her. Or even turned his charming smile on her.

He hadn't done any of those things. After turning his badge and gun over to Steve Drackett, he shook the man's hand and even made a joke.

Steve had looked relieved. Glad Joe had understood what needed to be done.

And Joe did understand. But he also had pushed his own feelings aside and given Steve what he needed.

That's what Joe did, Laura realized, for his job and also in his life. Read what people needed and gave them that. It was probably why he was such a good hostage negotiator.

After they'd left he'd told her the address of where his car was parked, still at Jessica Johannsen's house. He wanted Laura to drop him off there so he could make his way back home.

Despite everything that had happened between them, all the hurt he'd caused her six years ago, despite the fact that he'd probably slept with the gorgeous, perfect Cynthia and that his exes were dropping like flies, Laura could not send him home alone.

"We're at your house," Joe said as she pulled into her driveway. "I thought you were taking me to get my car."

"Change of plans. No one should have to be alone after the day you've had."

His gorgeous blue eyes became hooded. Laura could feel heat spreading through her at his look.

"Whoa, boy. This offer extends to my couch only. You need a friend. I can be that."

He stuck his bottom lip out in the most adorable pout she'd ever seen. She groaned inwardly. Having him spend the night here was such a bad idea.

"It's couch or nothing, Matarazzo."

He held his hands up in mock surrender. "Okay, couch."

She got him in, got them both fed and listened while he'd called someone and had them pick up his car from the crime scene. Then she gave him a pillow and blanket and the unopened toothbrush she had from her last dentist visit. She showed him the couch and said good-night.

She did it all trying her damnedest not to really look at him. Not to really notice the way his eyes followed her wherever she went. To definitely not think about how good the lovemaking had been between them six years ago.

She went into her bedroom, locking the door behind her. She knew that if Joe wanted in, that flimsy lock wouldn't keep him out.

She wondered if she even wanted it to.

JOE TOSSED AND turned most of the night.

His foot hung over the edge of Laura's couch, which was obviously not meant for someone of his height to sleep on. He was also thinking of Jessica and Sarah and their deaths. Of why someone would kill them.

He was thinking about how much it had

sucked when Steve had asked for his badge. How important working at Omega had become to him, even if—and it was clear by how easily Steve had suspended him today—Joe wasn't really part of the inner team.

But mostly he was thinking of Laura sleeping in her room right up the stairs.

There wasn't anything Joe wanted more than to go in there. To make love to Laura until he could forget about death and evil and blood.

But she deserved more than that. He had no doubt he could get past that small click of a lock he'd heard. He had no doubt he could seduce her into letting him stay in her bed tonight.

But as much as he wanted that, he didn't want that. Didn't want to use her in that way. At one time he would've thought about nothing except the pleasure both of them would gain if he ignored that tiny lock. Now he didn't want to risk what could possibly be a future between them for one night of sex. No matter how mind-blowing it might be.

Each moment seemed to drag into the next as Joe lay on the couch. He realized he needed Laura. Not for lovemaking, just to hold.

He needed to put his arms around her and thank the heavens that Laura was safe and sound and alive.

Suddenly, having distance between them, a wall—metaphorically and literally—separating them, seemed totally unacceptable. Joe wouldn't try to talk Laura into sex, but he'd be damned if he was going to stay out here when everything inside him demanded having her in his arms right now.

He was crossing the room before he finished the complete thought. His hand reaching for the doorknob was stopped by his phone buzzing from where it sat on the end table near the couch.

Joe almost ignored it. Wanted to ignore it. But

after everything that had happened in the last few days, he couldn't.

Olivia Knightley's name lit his screen when he picked it up. Another ex—a small-time actress he had dated for a few weeks about six months ago. He didn't know why she was calling in the middle of the night, but at least she was calling. That meant she was alive.

"Olivia?"

No response. Joe could tell someone else was on the line, but no one was talking.

"Olivia? It's Joe. Are you okay?"

Still silence. A few moments later the call ended.

Joe immediately redialed but it went straight to voice mail.

Damn it. Was Olivia in trouble? Should he call the police? Send them to her house just in case?

He was about to do just that when a text came through.

Sorry. I thought I could talk, but I couldn't.

Joe immediately texted back. Are you okay?

Yes, I'm fine. I have some info about the two women who died that I think you should see.

Why would Olivia have information about Jessica and Sarah?

Okay, fine. Can you send it? Or can we meet tomorrow?

It can't be sent. I have to show you in person. I'm leaving at dawn for a film shoot. It really needs to be tonight. Can you come now? I'm at my Colorado Springs house.

Joe didn't like anything about this, but was willing to do whatever it took to stop this killer.

Fine. He texted back. I'll be there in thirty minutes.

Chapter Nine

Olivia Knightley owned multiple houses. Two
of them in Colorado, since she loved to ski. Her
chalet in Vail was one of the loveliest Joe had
ever seen. You could ski right in and out of it.

Her other house, her personal home, was in
Colorado Springs, just north of Laura's. It was
small, in an unassuming neighborhood, and Joe
knew Olivia rarely invited people there. It was
her hideout. Somewhere the press didn't know
about.

Telling him to come to that house assured Joe
she was still alive. Very few people knew about
that house.

He and Olivia hadn't ended their relationship on very good terms. Mostly because of the woman sitting next to him in the car as he drove.

It hadn't taken long for the observant actress to realize the man in her bed had feelings for someone else. When Olivia had finally figured out it wasn't anyone current, anyone she could fight, but the memory of Laura that held Joe's heart, she'd cut him loose.

She'd been right to do that. Olivia deserved someone who could give her his full attention and heart. Joe's had already been partially taken.

Joe hadn't wanted Laura to come with him to Olivia's house for a couple of different reasons. First, it could be dangerous. Whatever information Olivia had, Joe knew the killer wouldn't be happy about it. Might go to great lengths to stop Joe from getting it. He didn't want to take the chance of putting Laura in harm's way.

Second, he didn't want to introduce her to an ex-girlfriend. That could be just as ugly.

If Laura hadn't had the keys to the car in her bedroom, Joe would've sneaked out without her being any wiser. But they had been in her room and she'd immediately awakened when he'd come in her bedroom door.

She hadn't thought he was looking for keys and would've been correct if he hadn't received Olivia's call and text. He'd quickly explained the situation.

"Are you sure we shouldn't call the cops?" she said now.

"We will if things look suspicious, I promise. Olivia values her privacy, especially at this house. She won't want anyone knowing about it."

Olivia would be happy to see Laura. To see that she'd been right all along about there being another woman in Joe's mind and heart. She'd spot Laura for what she was immediately.

Joe's.

For privacy's sake, Olivia's house was away from others in the neighborhood, surrounded by trees and at the end of a dead-end street. But beyond that it looked just like many of the other houses: upper-middle class, two stories, normal. Olivia loved to feel normal.

Joe parked on the side of the street. "I don't suppose I can talk you into staying in the car. Let me go see what Olivia knows and I'll be right out."

Laura was already opening her door. "Nope." She popped the *p* sound.

Joe wished he had the sidearm he'd been asked to turn in to Steve, or at least had made it home to get one of his other weapons. Walking up to Olivia's door he prayed it wouldn't be cracked open like Jessica's and Sarah's doors had been.

Thankfully it was closed. On it rested a note.

Joe, I'm up in my bedroom working on a script. Headphones. Just come on in.

"That's pretty stupid," Laura said. "What if it wasn't you coming to the door?"

Joe agreed but shrugged. "It's a pretty nice neighborhood, plus nobody knows she owns this house. She's pretty fanatic about her privacy when she's here. Her place to unwind, she calls it."

And at least the note meant Olivia was still alive. That's what mattered most.

"Sounds like you know a lot about her."

"We dated six months ago."

"Of course you did." Laura cocked her head sideways and studied him. "Are you still seeing each other now?"

"No."

"Does Olivia know that?"

"C'mon, Laura. You know I'm not as bad as the gossip rags make me out to be. I liked Olivia. We went out for a few weeks. But then it ended."

"Why?"

The same reason all of Joe's relationships had ended.

Olivia hadn't been Laura.

"Irreconcilable differences, I guess. We weren't what the other one wanted."

Laura didn't respond to that.

"Is she going to mind that I'm here? She's not going to be waiting for you naked or anything, is she?"

Joe remembered having the same thoughts about Jessica and Sarah.

He opened the door. "No, she won't be." He entered the house, Laura right behind him. "But if she is, cover my eyes and fight for my honor, okay?"

"How about if I cover my eyes and hit you in the head with a baseball bat?"

"That works, too." Joe wasn't totally sure she was joking and prayed Olivia would be fully clothed.

Various lights were on throughout the house as Joe led them to the stairs. He wondered if he should yell for Olivia so they didn't startle her.

"Where's her bedroom?"

"Up the stairs on the left."

Olivia's bedroom door was closed so Joe knocked, loudly.

Nothing.

His stomach clenched before remembering the note downstairs. Olivia had on headphones. He cracked open the bedroom door. "Olivia? It's Joe. I'm here with a friend of mine, Laura."

Still no answer. Joe flung the door open expecting the worst. He let out a sigh of relief when no one was dead in the bedroom. He walked fully inside, Laura right behind him.

"You okay?" She touched him on the back.

He blew out a breath in a shudder. "Yeah. It's just…" His words ran out.

"This situation was like the other two women's."

"Yeah. With both Sarah and Jessica I walked into the room and found them dead on the bed."

But Olivia wasn't. So where was she? Joe gave up on keeping quiet and began yelling for her.

Laura did the same. Joe searched in the bathroom and closet while Laura turned to look in the guest bedroom.

Laura's frightened cry had Joe running to her at the guest bedroom's door.

"What?"

She put out an arm to keep him from going any farther inside. "Joe, you've got to get out of here right now."

Joe felt sadness crash over him. "Oh no, not Olivia. She's dead?"

"Yes, definitely. I'm sorry."

Joe tried to enter the room but Laura pulled him back to her. "The best thing you can do for yourself is not get your DNA in this room."

Joe was looking at Olivia on the bed. Blood pooled around her naked form. Just like the other two women.

Laura's words barely registered, but her pull on him did. "What?"

She reached up and cupped his cheeks with

both hands, bringing her face close to his. His eyes finally focused on hers. "Someone is framing you, Joe. Two dead women who both knew you could possibly be a coincidence. But you finding the body of three of your ex-lovers? The police will arrest you for sure."

"But I didn't kill her. I didn't kill anyone." Joe felt like ramming his fist through a wall.

"I know. But someone has done an excellent job making it look like it was you."

"We can't just leave her here. We have to call the police."

Laura nodded. "We will but—"

She stopped her sentence as every light in the house switched off.

They reached for each other in the darkness.

"What just happened?" they both asked at the same time.

"Fuse blew?" Laura asked.

"Very convenient timing. Especially for us to have just discovered a dead body." Joe half expected to look out the window and see squad cars pulling up. It was like someone was trying to keep them here until the cops arrived and Joe could be blamed once again.

"I'm your witness this time. You were with me when we found Olivia. That will count for something."

"Let's go try to figure out the fuse situation."

"You go check it out. I'm going to stay here. I feel like something's going on, Joe. I don't want to leave the body."

Joe knew what she meant. He used the flashlight on his phone to hurry out to the garage, finding the fuse box and ripping it open. The box had all but exploded.

Someone had definitely messed with the fuse box, and recently.

Joe ran back to the door leading to the house but found it locked. He pushed against it with his shoulder, but it didn't budge.

Damn it. It must have automatically locked

when he came through. He jogged to the door leading to the outside and ran back around to the front of the house. As he stood in the driveway, a light in the upper window caught his attention. How could there be lights back on if the fuse box had been completely burned out?

It only took a slight flicker for him to realize it wasn't a light. The house was on fire.

Very close to where Laura had been standing.

Joe barreled through the front door. "Laura!" He ran toward the stairs then stopped as he saw fire swallowing the entire right side of the stairs.

Joe felt the tightness of the scar that covered part of his neck and back. He knew the agonizing sting of fire from his wounds last year.

"Laura!" He yelled again, but there was no response. The flames were becoming more intense now.

A fear like he'd never before experienced grasped Joe. Laura was somewhere in that fire.

Grabbing a blanket off the back of Olivia's

couch, he doused it under water in the sink and threw it around himself running past the flames on the stairs.

The smoke was thick on the second floor. Joe dropped low and belly-crawled toward the front of the house where he'd left Laura. Breathing was difficult, seeing even more so. He was almost crawling on top of her before he saw her lying totally still in the hallway.

"Laura." He shook her shoulder, coughing. "Laura, wake up."

She didn't move.

Joe knew he had to get her out of here, and he prayed she was just unconscious. He couldn't even think about anything further. He wrapped the blanket around her and began dragging her down the hall. He realized after a few moments she was helping him.

"Laura, are you okay?"

"Somebody hit me."

"What?" Had she said someone hit her?

"I was watching Olivia's body and someone hit me on the head from behind."

Someone was in the house with them.

Joe pulled Laura closer. "The house is on fire. We have to get out."

"Okay, I can crawl."

The fire was worse at the top of the stairs. Joe could feel the painful singe on the back of his neck.

They needed to get out right now.

Laura wrapped the damp blanket around them both as they half stumbled half ran down the stairs and through the hall. Fire licked toward them on all sides, but they kept moving so neither of them suffered burns as they made it out the front door.

Once outside, they both collapsed on the front lawn.

"Are you okay?" His voice came out as more of a hiss than anything else. He rolled over and touched her on the shoulder.

"Yes." Laura began to sit up. "Joe, someone was in the house with us. I thought you were coming up the stairs, and someone clocked me from behind."

"The fuse box had been almost completely destroyed. That's why all the lights had gone out. Then the door locked behind me so I had to run outside to get back in. That's when they got to you."

She gripped his hand. "Someone's going beyond just trying to frame you. It looks like someone wants to kill you. Maybe make it look like you killed Olivia, me and then yourself."

Terror gripped Joe at the thought that Laura could be right.

She began to stand. "We've got to get out of here. It won't take long before someone sees the fire and calls it in."

"You don't think I should stay and talk to the cops?"

"As your friend, I suggest you get as far away

from this crime scene as possible. As your lawyer, honestly, I would probably suggest the same. Nothing can be done for Olivia now, Joe." Her voice softened. "I'm sorry you lost another friend."

Another woman had died, and now there was no denying it was because of her connection with him. He looked at Laura. She could've been a target also. Could've easily died along with Olivia.

It wasn't in Joe's nature to run from a fight or from solving a crime. Especially since he had taken an oath to uphold the law when he'd joined Omega. But Laura was right. Staying here now wasn't going to do anything but get him arrested.

Sometimes you had to break the rules if it was the right thing to do.

He gripped Laura's hand and helped her up and to the car. They needed to get out of here.

He couldn't stop whoever was doing this if he was behind bars.

SHE WATCHED THE *house go up in flames, the beauty of the fire bewitching her. It had not taken Joe the way it was supposed to, but she could forgive it because of its loveliness.*

He brought the woman from the bank. Laura Birchwood, the lawyer. She thought Laura and Joe had just met last weekend but realized now that was incorrect. Joe had obviously known this woman much longer. Trusted this woman.

She'd made a mistake in thinking Joe would be distraught at the loss of his ex-lovers. Killing them—watching Joe find them—had not brought out in him the emotional response she had hoped for.

But today, watching as he realized Laura was *trapped in the burning house? That had been the reaction she'd been hoping to see with the others.*

Laura was the key.

And to think she'd almost killed her last week-

end when she ran Laura off the road. That would've been too quick, too painless.

Laura would play an important role in the revenge on Joe. Now she knew Laura's safety and well-being were the most important things to him.

Laura would die, but she would die in a way that would cause Joe the most pain. She would burn right in front of him.

But first Joe would fall.

Chapter Ten

After stopping at a twenty-four hour medical care clinic to make sure Laura's head wound and their smoke inhalation didn't require more serious attention, they'd returned to Laura's house. They'd both stripped naked in her garage, leaving their clothes—ruined by smoke—in there, and gone to separate showers. Laura didn't have anything that would fit Joe except a giant bathrobe belonging to her father. That would have to do until they could get him something else.

The pounding at her front door scared them both.

"You expecting anyone?" Joe whispered.

"Knocking on my door at seven o'clock in the morning? Um, no." She looked out her window and grimaced. "It's the police."

Joe muttered a curse.

"I knew they'd be looking for you, but had no idea it would be this soon." If they'd shown up fifteen minutes earlier, she would've had the smell of smoke still in her hair, a dead giveaway.

She turned to him. "Quick, go up in my room, stay out of sight."

"What are you going to do?"

"Talk to them. If they have a warrant to search my house, I won't be able to do anything. Otherwise, unless they see something suspicious, they can't come in. Don't come out." She pushed him toward her bedroom.

Pounding on the door resumed. Laura opened it. There stood Detective Thompson and two uniformed officers.

"Gentlemen, I have neighbors, if you don't mind. It's early."

"Ms. Birchwood, we're looking for Joe Matarazzo," Thompson said. "May we come in?"

"Do you have a warrant?"

Thompson's eyes narrowed. "No, ma'am."

Relief coursed through Laura. "Then no, gentlemen, you can't come in."

She began shutting the door, but Thompson held out a hand to stop it. Laura didn't want to add to their suspicions so she opened the door again. "Something else I can help you with?"

"Do you know where Matarazzo is?"

"Have you tried his house?" Laura sidestepped the question. "I'm his lawyer, Detective, not his girlfriend."

"Are you sure that's the case, Ms. Birchwood? We found these pictures online of the two of you together."

Thompson pulled out a half-dozen pictures he'd printed from the internet, passing them along to the other two officers to hold up as well as keeping two in his own hands.

She and Joe, six years ago, in full, unforgiving color. She found it difficult to look at the woman she'd been then. How much in love with him she'd been. The camera had captured it so perfectly.

She had to admit Joe looked pretty enthralled with her too in the photos. But she knew that had been a lie. Joe had never been captivated by her.

"Ancient history, gentlemen. Those photos were all taken half a dozen years ago."

Thompson collected the photos and got out another couple of prints. "How about these? They were taken last weekend if I'm not mistaken."

The photos someone had taken of them at dinner on Friday. The same ones that had reminded Laura why it was a bad idea to get involved again with Joe.

Glancing away from the pictures and back at Thompson, Laura realized she didn't need to lie. The truth would work best for her.

"It was dinner between two old acquaintances.

I'm sure you heard about the hostage situation at the bank in Denver on Friday. Joe Matarazzo got everyone out safely and we went out to celebrate a job well done. You might want to take that into consideration during your search for him. Joe is one of the good guys."

Thompson ignored the last part. "This picture doesn't look like dinner between two acquaintances."

He was right. Damned if Laura didn't have that same look in her eyes she'd had six years ago. And Joe looked just as enthralled.

Laura crossed her arms and leaned against her door. "Detective, I'm sure if you dig just a little deeper into our past relationship you'll see why I would have to be an absolute idiot to be harboring him now or not cooperating with you if I knew anything about his whereabouts."

That was the honest truth. She *was* an idiot.

"And why is that?"

"The gossip sites hated Joe and I together. Said

I wasn't attractive enough, polished enough, *sparkling* enough for someone like Joe. I'd be foolish to set myself up for that again."

Thompson shook his head. "Gossip reporters are vicious. No one takes them seriously."

"Joe Matarazzo took them seriously. Told me himself after a few months of dating that I wasn't the caliber of woman someone like him should be with. Why would I want to be around someone who doesn't think I am good enough for him?"

Thompson's eyes narrowed. Evidently Laura had just confirmed the detective's poor opinion of Joe. "I knew Matarazzo was an idiot. Has to be to say something like that. But you're still his lawyer?"

"He has no problem with my caliber as a lawyer. Plus, Joe is very wealthy. He made it worth my while to forget about past—" she shrugged "—misjudgments. On both our parts. So I helped him out yesterday. I imagine he'll get a full team of lawyers if all this continues. But there's nothing romantic between us and definitely nothing that would have him at my house at the crack of dawn."

"I see." Thompson nodded, but still didn't look completely convinced.

"Why are you looking for him so early? Something else must have happened or you would've charged him yesterday."

Laura knew it was risky bringing up the new murder, but it would be more suspicious if she didn't ask.

Thompson nodded. "There's been another murder. Someone else Matarazzo dated. Killer tried to cover it with a fire, but we got an anonymous tip-off that someone matching Joe Matarazzo's description was seen around the victim's house."

Laura's lips pursed. Anonymous tip-off could've been a neighbor. But it also could've been the true killer trying to make sure Joe was arrested since he'd made it out of the house alive.

Especially since no one mentioned her being there with him.

Thompson held up a picture of Olivia Knightley. "This was the lady who was murdered. Know her?"

Laura had to be careful here. "Not personally. She's an actress, right? Olivia something."

Thompson nodded. "Olivia Knightley. Matarazzo and Ms. Knightley dated six months ago."

"I wouldn't know anything about that. Now if you'll excuse me, I'm late for work."

"If Matarazzo does get in touch with you—since you're his lawyer and all—please call us. As his counsel I'm sure you would do the right, legal thing and tell him to turn himself in since there is a warrant out for his arrest."

"Of course."

"You should be aware that as an ex-lover of his, you are in danger, too. The only connection we've found between the three women so far is Matarazzo."

"I'll keep that in mind, Detective."

Thompson shot out his hand to keep her from shutting the door. "Matarazzo is a womanizer at best, Ms. Birchwood. I'm afraid he might also be a killer. Either way, women he's been intimate with keep winding up dead."

"Joe may be a jerk, but he isn't a killer, Detective. You need to keep searching for the real person committing these murders, not spend all your time looking for Joe."

Thompson's eyes narrowed and Laura feared she'd said too much. "Even if he isn't the killer, someone is targeting women he cares about, so that puts you in danger."

"Joe doesn't care about me. I'm just his lawyer and someone he knew a long time ago."

"I'm not so sure about that."

"Look at the women he dates and look at me, Detective. Olivia Knightley. Jessica Johannsen. They're stunningly gorgeous." Laura gestured to herself. She wasn't wearing any makeup, had her hair wrapped in a towel. "And look at me. No one could possibly think Joe and I belong in the same social realm together, much less that we could be a serious couple."

Thompson and the two other officers looked uncomfortable. She didn't blame them. They all knew what she said was the truth, even if they didn't want to admit it.

"Six years ago, I thought I had something special with Joe, then out of the blue he ended it with me because he figured out he could do better. He could find women superior in beauty, grace, wit and spark."

"Ms. Birchwood—"

"Well, three of those superior women are now dead. So I suppose I should be glad Joe found me so lacking then, or it might be me lying in the morgue right now."

Laura grabbed the door and pulled it partway shut.

"Joe and I aren't a good fit. That's what Matarazzo discovered years ago, and I agree whole-heartedly. I'm pretty sure I'm safe from whoever is killing the beautiful women Joe cares about."

Thompson nodded. "Again, I'm not so sure about that. Just be careful."

She murmured her thanks and shut the door, leaning her forehead against it.

Nothing like reliving all the painful details of your past to make a bad morning even worse.

Joe almost surrendered himself a half-dozen times while Laura spoke to Detective Thompson. It would've been easier than listening to all of that.

She was so wrong about how he'd felt six years ago. None of what she'd said to Thompson had been accurate. Not that Laura would know that.

Joe had been scared. He could admit that now. He'd been twenty-five and scared that he'd found the woman he wanted to spend the rest of his life with. Her looks, her *caliber*, had nothing to do with why he'd truly broken off their relationship.

Not that it made it any easier for her. To Laura he'd just been cruel.

Moving around the corner and seeing Laura leaning against the door destroyed Joe further. Before he could think better of it he walked over and wrapped his arms around her, pulling her back against his chest.

For just a moment she lay against him, her head resting back on his shoulder. A perfect fit, just like they'd always been. Then she stiffened and stepped away.

"I can't," she whispered. "Not right now. I don't want to touch you. To touch anyone. I just saw a dead woman lying five feet from me. Just washed smoke out of my hair from a fire that almost killed both of us. And my head is killing me."

"Laura—"

"Talking about the past, about what a fool I was? That was the last straw."

He had to try to make her understand. "That stuff I said six years ago, I didn't mean it."

She walked past Joe, careful not to touch him in any way. "You know what? It doesn't matter. You've got so many more important issues going on right now than our past."

She was right, but the pinched look on her face was still hard to swallow.

Laura walked into the kitchen. "You've got to get out of town. If Thompson doesn't have a warrant to search my house yet, he will soon. I'm not sure he believed me."

Laura's words about how she'd be a fool to get involved with Joe again had been pretty damn convincing, but he didn't point that out. "I don't want to run. I want to find out who's doing this and stop it."

"That's fine, but getting arrested isn't going to help with that plan." She rubbed a hand over her face. "I have a cabin in Park County about an hour west of here. It's in my mother's maiden name. No one would even tie it to me, much less you."

Joe shook his head. "No. I don't want to run."

"You're not running. You're retreating and re-grouping. Let me finish up work today and to-morrow, then I'll join you. We can try to get a handle on this."

He didn't want to go. Didn't want to take him-self out of where the action was. What good could he do at her cabin?

"What good will you do sitting in a cell?" It was as if Laura could hear his inner monologue.

He gripped the kitchen counter. "I feel use-less."

Her face softened. Laura couldn't stand to see other people in pain, even someone like him, who had caused her so much of it. "You're not useless. But we have to be strategic. And getting you out of Dodge is the best move right now."

She was right. But he still didn't like it.

"Okay. I'll go. But only if you promise to meet me at the cabin right after work tomorrow."

"I will. Hopefully, me going to work just like everything is normal will convince Thompson that we're not together. I'm sure he'll be watching me. They're probably watching my house, too, by the way. Just because they couldn't get inside doesn't mean they won't wait to snatch you as soon as you walk out."

"I'll use stealth—don't worry."

She smiled. "That robe is not going to get you any points in the nonconspicuous category."

"I'll handle clothes. Have something delivered." It was one of the perks of not having to worry about money.

All the money in the world couldn't bring back the women who had died. Joe planned to make sure it didn't happen to anyone else.

Chapter Eleven

Laura tried to act as normally as possible at work. That proved to be more difficult than she thought.

She shouldn't have been surprised. In the last twelve hours she'd seen a dead woman lying in a pool of her own blood, been knocked unconscious by an unknown assailant and had almost been killed in a fire. After that she'd lied, or at least intentionally misled, law enforcement officers, and harbored a fugitive.

That had all been before 8:00 a.m.

But all of that, as difficult to deal with as it

might be, wasn't what had her utterly unfocused today. Joe was what had her unfocused.

More specifically Joe looking so lost this morning and yesterday at Omega. His whole world was bottoming out beneath him and he didn't know what to do.

Laura wanted to help him. Wanted to wipe that look off his face. She was sure most of the world would agree that Joe Matarazzo's face needed to be plastered with an easygoing smile, not lines of worried exhaustion. A quick and charming wit was what the world expected of Joe.

He wanted to fix this, stop this killer. She knew if he could he would give his entire fortune to have the three women back safely. But neither his money nor his charm could mend this.

Joe had become a man of action. Wanting to do. Wanting to help. These women dying had hit him hard.

Omega Sector suspending him, despite it being

the best thing for the organization overall, also had him reeling.

Laura had to face the fact that Joe was no longer the man she'd known six years ago. He'd grown, matured. Had begun to put others' needs—even those of people he didn't know—before his own. Working in law enforcement had changed him.

It both pissed her off and caused her heart to flutter.

She had no idea what the hell she felt for Joe. For a woman used to knowing her own mind, it was frustrating.

She had to help Joe clear his name. The thought of Joe sitting in a cell, even temporarily, made her feel sick to her stomach. And she knew if Thompson found Joe he would definitely be detained, probably arrested and charged.

But right now Joe was safe at her cabin. She had planned to join him tomorrow, but she would go tonight instead. They needed to figure out the pattern behind the killings so they could get a lead on who was committing them.

Laura spent the last couple of hours of her day clearing her calendar and rescheduling meetings she'd had for the next day.

Yes, going to meet Joe tonight was better. He needed a friend. Laura could be that for him.

Just a friend.

She rolled her eyes. Yeah, right. She must be a glutton for punishment or something, but she couldn't stay away from him.

It was after seven when she finally finished everything she needed in order to clear her calendar for tomorrow. Everyone else was gone from the building. Laura would go home, grab a couple changes of clothes and meet Joe at the cabin.

And her changes of clothes would involve no sexy underwear whatsoever. Definitely not the red thong and matching bra she'd purchased a few weeks ago on a whim.

Because she definitely did not remember how partial he was to that color on her.

She walked into the parking garage her office shared with other offices on the block, taking the stairs down to the bowels where she was parked because she'd been so late getting here this morning.

A woman stood over in the corner, looking out at the lot. She smiled oddly at Laura so Laura gave her a little wave. Maybe she'd forgotten where she had parked. That had happened to Laura before, after a particularly long day.

Laura turned the corner toward her car. Besides the red lingerie, she would need her laptop so they could try to figure out the pattern the killer was using.

The brutal shove into a car caught her completely off guard. Laura was usually much more diligent when walking into the garage alone, but she'd been so caught up in getting to Joe she'd let her guard down.

She turned and saw a masked man. Laura tried to dive to the side, away from him, but he grabbed her arm.

"Where are you going, bitch?"

Remembering the other woman, Laura let out a scream, hoping she would call the police. Although by the time they got here it would be too late.

"So he cares about you, huh? We'll see how much," he muttered, wrapping his hand around her upper arm with bruising strength.

Was this guy talking about Joe? Was he the one who had killed the other women?

Laura began fighting with a renewed frenzy. She would not let this man kill her and frame Joe for it.

She threw her arms and legs around wishing she had more background in self-defense. Her captor grunted as some of her frantic blows connected with sensitive places. He cursed and backhanded her. She fell against another vehicle.

"Let's go, Max. Hurry up!" Another masked man in an SUV parked toward the exit yelled.

Laura tasted blood in her mouth as she got up from the hood of the car where she'd fallen. Out of the corner of her eye she saw the woman again, just watching, too afraid to get involved.

The large man grabbed her by the hair and began dragging her toward the other van. She punched at him but it wasn't enough to stop him. She dropped all her weight to the ground crying out at the stinging pain in her scalp when he didn't let go. She couldn't let him get her in the vehicle.

"Help me with her," he called out to the other guy.

A few seconds later she felt the other guy grab her legs. Laura screamed, trying to draw any attention to herself, until a meaty fist covered her mouth.

She bit it.

The man yelled and she saw fury burn in the

eyes visible through the black ski mask. She braced herself for the fist flying toward her face.

Instead she and her two captors went flying to the ground as a huge force knocked into them.

Joe.

He kicked the guy who had been holding her legs in the jaw and sent him flying back. Laura scurried out of the way as the first man rolled with Joe on the cement, both of them giving and receiving bone-crunching blows.

Joe obviously knew what he was doing. These weren't just lucky punches he was getting in. And even with both of them rolling on the ground he effectively blocked many of the attacker's—a man much bigger and meatier—blows.

Laura scrambled to her feet and saw the second man rushing back at Joe with a knife in his hand.

"Joe, behind you. A knife!"

Her words gave him just enough time to spin

around, the blade catching him in his shoulder rather than the middle of his back. Laura heard a sickening snap and a high-pitched scream from the attacker as Joe made short work of the knife in the other man's hand, breaking his wrist and recovering the weapon himself.

This was a Joe she had never seen before. Had never known existed. Would've sworn didn't exist if she couldn't see him with her own eyes.

There was no carefree in him now, no charm. Just deadly intent and overwhelming force.

Both men began backing away now that Joe had not only proved himself capable of handling them, but had a weapon. Within moments they were fleeing to their vehicle and speeding out of the parking garage.

Joe rushed to her, touching her lip gently where the guy had hit her. "Are you okay?"

Laura's short laugh had a bark of hysteria. "Me?" She looked at his arm where blood was dripping through the sleeve of his blue shirt.

"You're the one bleeding. We need to get you to a hospital."

"No, I'm fine. Plus a hospital might ask too many questions. We've got to go."

She let him lead her to her car. "Why are you even here? I thought you went to the cabin."

"I couldn't do it. Couldn't run, leaving you alone. What if one of Olivia's neighbors had reported that they remembered seeing us *both* outside her house? The cops could've come back and arrested you. There was no way I would let that happen."

She nodded.

"Not to mention someone killing people linked to me." He gestured vaguely toward where the masked guys had driven off.

Joe opened the passenger door of the car for her, but she stopped, leaning against the side of the vehicle, closing her eyes, needing a minute. Trying to stop the spinning in her head, not just from the blows.

Joe's hand softly cupped her cheek. "Are you sure you're okay?"

"Those were the guys trying to frame you."

"I know."

"They were going to take me and kill me like the others. You would've found me dead at my house."

Joe didn't say anything, just pulled her closer to him. She breathed in his scent, feeling his lips at her temple.

"We need to leave," Joe finally said.

Laura nodded. The guys might come back, or the police. Either way, staying here was dangerous.

"We'll both go to the cabin."

THEY DROVE STRAIGHT out of town. Joe ripped a strip off one of the shirts he'd purchased and had delivered to Laura's house this morning. It stemmed the bleeding from the cut on his shoulder. Not getting stitches would probably leave a scar, but a hospital wasn't worth the risk.

They stopped only once on the way to the cabin, at a super center to get a first aid kit, some clothes for Laura and enough food for while they holed up and tried to figure out who was trying to frame Joe. The cashier had given the two of them quite a look, for once not because she recognized Joe, but because she was worried he was some backwoods husband beating on his wife.

Joe couldn't blame the cashier. Laura looked exhausted. Her lip was swollen from the punch she'd taken, her hair and makeup were a mess. Her eyes dull and unfocused.

So unlike Laura.

He paid in cash and put the bags in the cart, grabbing Laura's hand. It was icy. He rubbed her arms up and down, feeling her coldness even through her blouse. He bent down so his eyes were right in front of hers. "You okay?"

She blinked and focused on him. "Yeah, I just…" She shrugged. "I'm sorry."

"Let's get you to the cabin." He wanted to take off his jacket and give it to her, but his blood-soaked sleeve would be too memorable. They had already drawn enough attention. He tucked Laura to his side and pushed the cart out with one hand.

Laura's cabin on Lake George, fifty miles west of Colorado Springs stood private and simple. She was right; no one would look for them here. Joe led her into the cabin, checking it thoroughly himself first, and sat her on the couch. When he came back in from carrying the bags she was still sitting exactly where he'd placed her.

This wasn't good.

He knew she was exhausted, in pain—she'd taken two hits to the head in the last twenty-four hours—probably hungry and definitely in shock. If it wasn't for his training with Omega, Joe would probably be all those things too.

He saw bottles of alcohol on an antique tray by the kitchen table. A good shot of quality scotch would probably do them both good. Hell, a finger of *any* scotch would do them good. He poured two glasses and sat down next to Laura.

"Here, drink this."

She did without comment, which just confirmed how far gone she was.

The strong burn pulled her back. "What *is* that?" she sputtered.

Joe grinned. "Whiskey."

"I think enough people have tried to kill me today without you joining the club, thank you very much." Coughs racked her body.

"Just call it liquid fortification. You were looking a little hollow there for a second."

She nodded. "I was feeling a little hollow."

He slipped off his jacket and grabbed the first aid kit. Laura helped him clean and wrap the cut on his shoulder that thankfully wasn't too deep and had long since stopped bleeding. It hurt now, but it wasn't going to cause him any permanent issues.

Joe put the first aid supplies on the side table then leaned all the way back against the couch next to Laura. "Hell of a day, hasn't it been?"

"Where did you learn to fight like that?"

"Not everybody liked rich kids as I was growing up. It was either have full-time security following me around middle school or learn how to protect myself."

"Did your middle school moves include learning to break someone's wrist?"

Joe was glad to see the liquor was working. Laura didn't seem nearly as brittle as she had before. He pulled her so she was resting next to him, back against the couch.

"When I started working at Omega Sector I ended up learning a lot more defensive and offensive tactics. Weapons training, close-quarter fighting. The whole works."

"Well, it showed today."

"Thank God for that."

She let out a huge yawn and he slid to the side of the couch, pulling her with him, until they were both lying flat, her tucked against him. He felt her stiffen.

"You're okay. I'm okay. Let's just rest," he murmured. "I don't need anything you're not willing to give me. I just want to hold you and know you're alive."

Because she very easily might not have been. Listening to his instincts—staying in town rather than going to the cabin—had never served him better than it had today.

He felt her relax and drift off to sleep. Good, she needed it. He would just hold her here while she slept.

It was more than he'd ever thought he'd get again, anyway. He'd take it.

He slept also. He knew he did because when he woke Laura's soft sweet lips were on his.

"We didn't die," she murmured against his

mouth. "When that guy came at you with the knife I thought he would kill you."

Joe reached down and grabbed Laura's hips, pulling her more fully on top of him. There. Touching him from head to toe. That's how he wanted her.

"When I came around the corner and saw those two guys trying to carry you off—" he broke away and whispered "—my heart stopped."

"Make love to me, Joe." Her fingers were already loosing the top button of her shirt.

"Laura." He brought his lips back to hers, rubbing his hands up and down her spine. "I want to make sure this is what you really want. This has been a crazy day. We don't have to do this."

She rolled her hips against his. "Are you suggesting you don't want to?"

He half groaned, half laughed. "That is obviously not the case."

"Then what's the problem? I've crawled on top of you. I'm unbuttoning my blouse. I'm feeling pretty confident about what I want. And I'm definitely not drunk if that's your concern."

What was his problem? Why was he not helping her with said blouse and moving things right along? He definitely wanted to.

He cupped both sides of her head and brought her face up so he could see her. Hazel eyes, clear and focused, stared back at him. Her little chin jutted out as if she was daring him.

To stop or go further, he didn't know.

He realized the problem. He didn't want this to just be let's-celebrate-we're-alive sex. He wanted it to mean something to her. An emotional connection between the two of them. Because as much as he wanted her—which was pretty much more than his next breath—he didn't want to jeopardize a possible future with her for a few hours of passion.

Oh, how the mighty Casanova had fallen.

He could feel Laura start to stiffen, true doubt entering her eyes. It gutted him, the thought that she doubted his desire for her. Laura wanted him. He would take her any way he could get her.

And pray it would be enough to tie her to him more completely.

He wrapped his arms around her, sitting up so quickly a little squeak escaped her. He swiveled and sat back against the couch so she was straddling his hips. He tilted his head and took her mouth.

He stopped thinking, and just allowed himself to feel. To sink into that soft, wet mouth. To trace it with his tongue, tease her warm lips apart and explore.

He kept the pace slow and easy, wanting to enjoy, to savor. Laura unbuttoned and peeled his shirt off him, careful of the wound on his shoulder. He made short work of her blouse before bringing her back in for a kiss.

The pace was much more frantic now. She gripped his waist, tugging him to her.

He couldn't breathe for the pleasure of it. All

he could do was get closer. Her body was too far away even though they were plastered to each other.

He wrapped his arms around her hips and stood, still holding her to him.

"Where's the bedroom?" His words came out as a growl against her lips.

"Two rooms, both have the same size beds. Take your pick. But be quick about it."

He smiled, carrying her across the room to the first door he came to.

"This better not be a closet, or I'm not going to make it to a bed."

She giggled and he reached down and gently bit the juncture of where her neck met her shoulder. Her laugh turned into a sigh. She wrapped herself more tightly around him.

It was a bedroom. Within moments he had her on the bed, both of them naked. And he proceeded to lose himself in the woman he'd never been able to fully get out of his heart.

Chapter Twelve

The next morning Laura awoke to the smell of coffee and an indentation in the mattress where Joe had recently lain.

What had she done?

Besides having had the best night of lovemaking since…

Since she and Joe had broken up six years before.

She groaned into her pillow.

The physical side of their relationship had never been a problem. As a matter of fact, no side of their relationship had been a problem. Or at least Laura had thought as much.

Until the day Joe dumped her out of the blue.

"I can almost see your brain working at a million miles an hour." Joe walked into the room holding coffee.

He was so sexy, so rumpled and casual. Handing her a perfect cup of coffee.

Laura could see so easily why she had fallen in love with him before. She would be a fool to let herself make the same mistake twice. She should not forget that Joe—despite all the ways he seemed to have grown—could change his mind and decide out of the blue again that he didn't want her anymore.

She couldn't survive her heart shattering twice.

"Just trying to figure out how we're going to get out of this mess unscathed."

Joe's eyes narrowed slightly and Laura knew he wasn't sure if she was referring to the bedroom situation, the police situation or both.

Good. Let him wonder. She was wondering, too.

"We've got to figure out who's setting me up."

"Okay." Laura took a sip of her coffee then set it on the nightstand. She ran out into the living room, aware she was only wearing one of his T-shirts. It was too big on her, but she was still conscious of how much of her legs was exposed.

She grabbed her legal pad and pen from her bag and came back to the bedroom. "We need a list. 'Who would want to hurt Joe?'"

"I don't think I like this list."

"We can call it 'people who think Joe is an ass.' Is that better?" She smiled innocently.

He rolled his eyes, shaking his head. "I think the first one will suffice."

They worked on the list for the next couple of hours, and while they fixed and ate breakfast, forming two basic categories: people he'd helped put in jail and his ex-lovers. She didn't make him name all his ex-lovers—because seriously her heart couldn't take it—just people with whom he'd had relationships that ended badly. They'd both realized quickly that Laura would be at the top of that list so they'd moved on to the people he'd put in jail.

"Sometimes people feel like I fed them untruths. I try not to lie to hostage-takers, but my first priority is always getting everyone out alive. If I suggest no jail time will be involved and they believe me and surrender..." He shrugged.

"It can't be anyone from inside jail. It has to be someone who's out."

"It could be someone connected to someone I put in jail, but I can't remember all those names on my own. We're going to need my case files from Omega."

Laura put down her notepad. "Will they give them to you?"

Joe shrugged. "I don't know. I'm not going to ask. We'll need to sneak them out."

Why wouldn't he ask? Asking seemed much simpler than sneaking. "Steve Drackett seemed pretty reasonable. If you tell him we think—"

"No."

Laura waited for the rest of the explanation but none came.

Good thing she was a lawyer and talking sense into people was sometimes part of her job. "Joe, from everything I know and have seen of Omega Sector, it's a pretty tight-knit group. You are part of the team. Steve will help if you ask him."

"Things aren't always as they seem. There is a team, but I'm more of an outsider. Trust me— they don't want to be a part of this problem, especially now that a third woman connected to me is dead. I'm sure Steve would rather I just use my money to help get myself out of this mess."

She reached for his arm but he slid away.

"Joe—"

He reached forward and kissed her on the forehead before standing and walking across the room. "It's not a big deal, seriously. It's not like they dislike me or anything. I'm just not part of the inner core."

"That's not how it looked to me."

"Like I said, sometimes things aren't always the way they look."

She wanted to argue but didn't have the facts to back up her case. "Okay, so we have to sneak them out. Great, breaking more laws. How will we get in?"

"My ID probably won't work right now. Or will at least alert security if I enter the building since I'm on suspension. The files are in a relatively unsecured section in a different building, but getting in the front door is the problem."

"Do you have a plan?"

"Yeah." He grimaced. "But you're not going to like it."

JOE WAS RIGHT; she didn't like his plan.

They were back in Colorado Springs, at a bar not far from Omega Sector headquarters. It was actually called Barcade—as in, bar and arcade mixed—and it was chock full o' geeks. The group of particular interest to Joe were the geeks who worked at Omega Sector. Data-entry people, if Laura understood correctly.

They all knew Joe and had fallen over themselves when he'd shown up at "their" bar. Evidently he'd been invited a few times but this was the first time he'd shown up. They'd either not heard the news about him being suspended or totally didn't care.

Joe was talking to them like they were the bestest buddies he'd ever had. Not that he was being insincere—no, Joe genuinely liked people. Liked listening to them, liked talking to them. He liked *these* people.

But he had an agenda. He was using them to get what he wanted. The fact they would've given it to him willingly was irrelevant.

Three rounds of drinks and an untold number of jokes, laughs and stories later, Joe and Laura walked out of Barcade, two "borrowed" Omega IDs in Joe's back pocket.

The data-entry gang was going to see a movie.

Joe told them he and Laura already had plans, but insisted they wanted to meet up with them afterward for a nightcap.

So he could slip their IDs back in their pockets, although Joe didn't tell them that.

Admiration and disgust warred within Laura as she and Joe walked the blocks to Omega after seeing the gang off to their movie.

"You're mad," Joe said, not slowing their brisk pace.

"*Mad* isn't the right word."

"Those guys are low clearance. No one could get into any highly secured part of Omega Sector with their IDs. So there's no real security breach here. But it will get us what we need."

"I'm not mad about security clearance."

"Your eyes tell a different story."

Laura took a deep breath. "I'm not mad. It's just…those people trusted you. Really thought you were interested in them."

Joe stopped walking and turned to face Laura,

grabbing her arm. "Wait a second, I *was* interested in them. They're an interesting group. A little geeky, but not bad overall."

"You were only talking to them because you wanted to shoplift their IDs. Only laughing and pretending to like them because you needed something from them."

He looked affronted. "That's not true. I walked into that bar because of needing their IDs, but talking to them, listening, laughing—that wasn't fake. They're good people."

"Have you ever hung out with them before?"

Now he looked a little sheepish. "Not here, outside of work. But I've talked to them inside Omega."

Laura shrugged. It was a fine line. But she realized it was a line he walked all the time in his job as a hostage negotiator. He got people to trust him for a living. Got them to talk, listened to them, made them feel special.

"Laura, this was the quickest, least painful

way to get us into Omega. None of them are hurt in the process and you and I are able to get the info we need to stop another woman from getting killed."

"You used them, Joe. Plain and simple."

Joe's face fell, became shuttered. Obviously he hadn't seen it that way.

She wasn't trying to hurt his feelings, but damn it, it sucked to be used. She knew.

And when had this become about her?

"You know what?" Laura started walking again. "Forget I brought it up. You're right—getting the info, saving women's lives is more important than how we get the info."

"Laura—"

"Let's go. We've got to be back at the bar by the time they're done with the movie."

Laura caught Joe's gaze out of the corner of her eye. He had more he wanted to say, but just nodded. They walked in silence the rest of the way to Omega. Joe turned toward a side entrance rather than the front door.

"Records are held in this section. It's not connected to the regular building. No security guards, but you need an active ID to enter." Joe's voice was no-nonsense.

"Okay."

"Try to look down as we enter because there are security cameras. I took IDs from one guy and one woman, the two whose features are most similar to ours, but we still don't want to be looking at the camera as we walk in."

"Do you even know the names of the people you took the IDs from?" Were they just two more people Joe used and discarded?

Joe stopped again. He held the cards out to Laura without looking at them. "Cory Gimbert and Carolyn Flannigan. She's pretty new, so I have to be honest, I don't know how long she's worked here. Cory's been here two years. We both love *Star Wars* and he emails me whenever new rumors or trailers or anything hit the web. We're buds."

His eyes were hard when he handed Laura Carolyn's card. "Ready?"

Laura nodded. She'd hurt his feelings. She hadn't even been aware of the level of buried hostility she'd felt for Joe. But evidently it was high.

Now wasn't the time to deal with it. "Yes."

Joe walked up to an unassuming back door, nothing like the front door with its guards and weapon scanners. He scanned his ID then walked through. Laura did the same.

He waited for her inside the door, body held at a slightly odd angle. She realized he was protecting them both from the eye of the camera.

"Do the cameras have sound?"

"Not that I know of. I have a buddy in security I chat with from time to time—that's how I know about the security camera. But he didn't mention sound."

Another buddy. Laura was beginning to see a pattern. A lot of buddies. No real friends.

They kept walking down the hallway. "Hard copies of closed case files will be down here in written records storage." He led them quickly to a door.

"Okay, you take the top half of the list, I'll take the bottom. I wish we had time to scan the files and leave them, but to be honest, I'm not sure how long we have."

"So we'll just take the files?"

Joe shrugged. "Sometimes it's better to ask forgiveness than permission. If we use these to stop the real killer, I don't think anyone is going to question our methods. Besides, they're all cases I worked. Technically I have access to them whenever I need them."

If he wasn't suspended.

"Okay, let's get started." There were nearly twenty cases on the list Joe had texted her. Joe used Cory's ID to enter the written records room, which was exactly what it sounded like: rows of filing cabinets holding printed records of cases Omega had been involved with.

"I don't have any friends who work here," Joe said almost apologetically. "I don't know how their filing system works."

"Let me see if I can figure it out." Laura used Carolyn's ID card to log in to the computer at the front of the room. It seemed to be a closed system, low-level clearance like everything else in this section of Omega, but it got them the info they needed.

"I can run a search with your name and the last three years." She printed the paper listing where the files were held.

Joe took half. "Okay, let's get them and get out of here."

Finding the files wasn't difficult once they understood the system, but it became obvious they were going to have quite a lot to go through back at the cabin. After, of course, they met Cory and Carolyn and the gang for one more drink so Joe could slip their IDs back from wherever he'd gotten them.

"Ready?"

Laura handed him the files she had collected and he slipped them all into his backpack. It was full. "We've got a lot to go through."

"I just hope it will get us the answers we need. Or at least somewhere to start looking."

Joe turned and opened the door to the hallway so they could exit.

There stood Steve Drackett, Joe's boss, waiting for them.

Chapter Thirteen

Damn it.

Steve had a reputation for never leaving Omega, but it was ten-thirty on a Friday night. What the hell was he doing here?

"Hey, Steve." Joe had no idea how he was going to talk himself out of this one. He was about to go to jail.

"Joe." Steve nodded. "Ms. Birchwood."

"Director Drackett. Good to see you again." Laura gave Steve a professional smile as if they hadn't just been caught sneaking into a law enforcement building, while on the run from law enforcement, to steal law enforcement files.

Steve leaned against the door frame. "I'm sure you're aware that another woman—Olivia Knightley—was killed yesterday. Another ex-girlfriend of yours if I'm not mistaken."

Damn it. "Steve, I—"

"And with that third girlfriend being killed, there is officially a warrant out for your arrest."

"I didn't kill them, Steve. I swear."

Steve continued as if he hadn't heard Joe. "Of course, as a law enforcement entity, I set our Omega computers to ping me if something with your name came up in any computer. Credit card use, someone spotting you and posting on their blog, arrest reports. So it struck me as weird when someone was searching your name here in my very own Omega Critical Response Division building."

Joe saw Laura wince from the corner of his eye. If she hadn't been so logical and efficient at getting them the files, Steve wouldn't know they were here.

Joe tried to sort the options out in his head. He could fight his boss, try to get himself and Laura out of the building. But Steve was no old man—forty or forty-one at the most—and despite not taking part in active missions anymore, still kept himself in top shape. He'd probably forgotten more fighting tricks than Joe had ever learned.

Joe would have to talk his way out of this. "Steve—"

Steve held up his hand. "I'm going to assume those are case files in your backpack."

"They are." Joe nodded.

"I will therefore assume that you are not the person killing these women and that you're looking at past cases for suspects."

Steve actually believed him? "Yes, that was our plan."

"I'd like to assume that this elaborate plan to sneak into the building and take these files was due to some misguided thinking on your part to protect me and Omega from ramifications with other law enforcement agencies."

"Well, yes, actually. I didn't want to—"

Steve didn't let him finish. "But what I really think is the issue is that you didn't think we would have your back."

Joe sighed. "I didn't want to drag you or anybody else into this mess. *My* mess."

"Looks like you were willing to drag Laura into the mess, as you call it."

That was true. But not because he'd wanted to. But because… Hell, Joe didn't know why he'd been willing to drag Laura into it.

"You trust her." Steve finished the thought for him. "And you don't trust your colleagues at Omega."

"That's not true. I put my life in their hands all the time."

"Because that's their job, and your job, and everyone is damn good at it. But you don't trust them to really see you as part of the team and to have your back when the going gets tough."

Because he *wasn't* really part of the team. Joe had always known that. Everyone was friendly; everyone joked with him, and even invited him out when they were getting together. But inside, Joe had always known that they thought of him as different. That his money, his pseudocelebrity status, made him different in their eyes.

That they thought of him as a great guy, laid-back, fun. But not as a member of the team.

"I got suspended, Steve. Remember that?"

Steve's eyes narrowed. "That is standard procedure when someone is being investigated for something as serious as murder. For your protection and Omega's."

Joe knew that. Logically, he knew that. But it had still stung.

Steve shifted. "Let me ask you something. How long do you think it took me to find that cabin of Ms. Birchwood's?"

Joe heard Laura's sharp intake of breath.

"Once there was a warrant out for your arrest, Omega was legally compelled to help find you. Detective Thompson was the first person here demanding info. It was a damn shame a virus ate all the information we had about you and Laura."

Steve was protecting him.

"How long do you think you could hide if I was using all Omega's resources to find you? Maybe if you took your money and got out of the country you'd be safe. But you didn't do that."

"Because I didn't kill those women." Joe felt Laura's hand slip into his. It meant everything to him.

"Hell, Joe, I never for a single second considered that you killed those women. It's my job to look at every possibility when it comes to a crime and I never considered you a viable option. Nobody here did."

Joe wasn't sure what to say. He'd obviously misjudged his boss. "Steve—"

"Take your files and get out of here. Find out who's doing this and let's stop him. I need my team back together."

Joe nodded and put his hand at Laura's back leading her down the hall.

"And give those kids back their IDs," Steve called out after them. "Tell them to be more careful or I'm going to fire their asses."

Laura was, in Joe's humble opinion, having way too much fun with her legal pad and the list of "who thinks Joe is an ass." She'd brought up the ex-lovers again, although given that those were the people who were dying, that wasn't likely. Plus, Laura pointed out it made the list too long, so they were better off just dealing with something more manageable.

Joe responded to that by backing Laura up against the wall and kissing her until neither of them could breathe. At first she'd been stiff, but had turned soft and compliant after just a few moments.

She was still mad, Joe knew, about Cory's and Carolyn's IDs. Laura's practicality had won out overall—she had to admit it had worked and returning the IDs had been even easier than taking them—but she hadn't liked it.

She thought Joe was using the techs. And in that case, yes, Joe could admit he was. But it wasn't his normal practice. He normally didn't need people to get what he wanted. Hell, if he wanted something he could usually buy it.

He wanted Laura's trust, but money couldn't buy that. Tonight's stunt had just pushed him a couple steps backward from winning her trust.

First he'd take care of a maniac, then he'd concentrate on showing Laura she could trust him.

Now they were looking at the case files, studying the people Joe had a hand in putting behind bars.

There were a lot.

Joe grimaced, looking up from a case three years old. "Some of these people are still in prison. We can rule them out."

"Unless it's a member of their family trying to get revenge. We know there are two men involved, from the guys who tried to take me from the parking garage."

"Well, there's Ricky and Bobby, aka, the Goldman brothers, Mitchell and Michael. But they're definitely still in lockup. Although I suppose they could be out on bail."

"One guy in the parking garage called the other guy Max. So it can't be the Goldman brothers."

"He said Max? Are you sure?" Joe found the Ricky/Bobby file and opened it.

"Pretty positive, why?"

"Well, there are actually four Goldman brothers. Mitchell and Michael were the ones from last Friday, and were evidently pretty irritated at me that they were arrested."

"Why? They were the ones who took sixteen

people hostage and assaulted the manager and assistant manager."

Joe shrugged. "Evidently they thought that having a good reason for taking people hostage gave them a free pass."

Laura shook her head. "Wow."

"So yeah, they're threatening revenge and all that stuff. I thought I would worry about that when they got out of jail in three to five years. But, interestingly, they have two other brothers."

Laura rolled her eyes. "Great. Just what the world needs."

"Brothers' names are Melvin and Max."

That got her attention. "Max?"

"Interesting, isn't it, that the murders started a couple days after the Goldman brothers were arrested and that someone named Max tried to kidnap you, presumably to kill you?"

"Do you really think it's them?"

Joe got out his phone and made a call. Sometimes having a lot of money at your disposal helped. During his past few years in law enforcement Joe had made a lot of contacts, some that worked inside the law and some who worked outside it.

Deacon Crandall did both.

"Deacon, this is Joe Matarazzo."

"Joe." He heard Deacon yawn. "It's seven o'clock on a Saturday morning. And, btw, you're wanted by law enforcement."

"Yeah, well, that's because my exes keep showing up dead."

"Lucky bastard. I wish some of my exes would do the same. What can I do for you?"

Deacon didn't ask Joe if he'd murdered the women. Joe didn't know if that was because he trusted Joe was innocent or he just didn't care.

"I need you to find a Melvin Goldman in the Colorado Springs area. Shouldn't be hard. He would be brother of Max, Michael and Mitchell Goldman."

"Okay. What do you want me to do with Mr.

Goldman, whose parents didn't know the alphabet contained other letters besides *m*?"

"I need you to find out if he has a broken arm. If you happen to see Max Goldman, he probably will have a pretty bruised face."

"Okay. Do I need to pick them up?"

"Nope, just let me know if they have those wounds and their whereabouts. If so, I'll want to talk to them myself. And Deacon, I'll pay you triple your normal rate if you can get me the info in the next hour."

"You can expect my call."

An hour later Joe and Laura had already received Deacon's call. Not just a call but photos of both Max and Melvin. Sure enough Melvin's arm rested in a sling and Max's face still held bruises from Joe's fists. Deacon sent them an address where the brothers were lying low.

"I'm going to talk to them." Joe grabbed his coat.

"I'm going with you."

Joe was torn. He didn't want to leave Laura alone, but he also didn't want to bring her into a potentially dangerous situation.

"I'm not staying here in the cabin, Joe. Not when something could happen to you while you're in town. You might need me as your lawyer."

He needed her as so much more than that.

"Fine."

"Do you want to call any of your Omega people? For backup, or whatever?"

Joe hesitated. He knew what Steve had said last night about being part of the team. But it was one thing for his boss to believe him, another thing for all his colleagues to just trust Joe was telling the truth when all the evidence said otherwise. He was better off not even asking.

"No. I'm going in alone."

"What about what Steve said?"

"Steve is one thing. My actual colleagues? I can't be sure they're not going to choose the job over me. I wouldn't blame them for choosing the job over me."

Laura shook her head. "I think you're wrong."

Joe shrugged. He couldn't chance it. He shook his head. "Alone. I took the Goldman brothers once. I can deal with them again."

Chapter Fourteen

Laura didn't like the thought of Joe going in alone to question the Goldman brothers, but he seemed adamant about not calling any of his colleagues.

She realized for all of his money, his nice cars, vacation houses and gadgets, Joe Matarazzo was essentially alone. He'd be the first one to laugh off her words with a joke about poor little rich boys. But that didn't make it any less true.

It wasn't that Joe didn't trust other people, it was that he just didn't want to put them in a position where they had to state outright that they trusted him.

His easygoing nature and charm were what made him such a critical part of the Omega team, but it was also why he thought no one took him seriously. That no one would take his side in this situation.

That no one trusted him. When they all would, Laura knew.

Of course, she felt a little hypocritical because Laura didn't trust him, at least personally. She was still afraid he would turn around at any moment and say that now that he'd thought about things again, his initial inclinations had been correct and they really weren't from the same worlds.

Truly, it was only a matter of time before he said that again. Laura knew it had to be true.

"Laura, I've been thinking." Joe's eyes were on the road. His voice somber.

She felt her heart catch. Was this it already? The last two nights had been amazing, but sex had always been amazing for them. Was Joe already coming to his senses?

This time she wasn't going to let it destroy her.

"It's okay, Joe. Just say it."

Now he glanced over at her, brows furrowed. "Just say what?"

Laura cleared her throat. "You know, whatever it is you're thinking."

She could take it. Yeah, her heart would crack, but it wouldn't shatter like last time.

"I was thinking there should probably be a third group on the 'who thinks Joe is an ass' list."

Okay, that wasn't what she had been expecting. She struggled to regroup mentally. "Okay. Who?"

"Families of people I've killed."

She could feel the shock rock through her. "*What?* You killed someone? Who did you kill?"

"There have been innocent people who have been killed because I couldn't make enough

headway with the hostage-takers who had them."
She could hear the pain in his voice. The guilt.
The doubt.

"But that doesn't mean you killed them."

He shrugged. "It might be considered close
enough by some grieving family members."

"Have many people been killed in hostage situations?"

"No. The SWAT team at Omega and I have a
great record. Almost anyone I haven't been able
to talk down they've been able to take out."

"But not always."

Joe shook his head. "Last year around this time
was a particularly bad situation. Guy had a hand
grenade. Killed four people. Almost killed me."

"Are those the burn scars on your neck and
back?"

His hands tightened noticeably on the steering wheel. "Yeah. A much smaller price to pay
than what the four hostages did. They all died."

"You know that wasn't your fault, right? The

man with the grenade, the one who took the people in the first place. He was at fault."

"It was a guy who'd gotten fired. Came back into his office and walked into the conference room. I got him to release six people. But he wouldn't let his bosses or office mate leave. He said they were the ones directly responsible."

"Joe—"

"I should've known he wanted blood. He let the other people go too easily and I thought I could handle him. The SWAT team thought they could take him out in time if needed, but none of us saw the hand grenade."

Laura knew there were no words that could make this any better for Joe. She reached over and touched his knee.

He glanced at her briefly before looking back to the road. "Anyway, that should probably be another list of people who hate me. People who lost loved ones because of my mistakes."

"I'm sure they don't hate you."

"I think I might if I was them. I met with the families after last year's incident. Tried to give them as much closure as I could, explain what happened as best as I was able."

"None of them blamed you, Joe. I know it."

He reached down and grabbed her hand. "One of the men who died—the office mate—was about to become a father for the first time. His wife was three months pregnant when he was killed."

The anguish was clear in his voice.

"That kid—it was a little girl—is never going to know her father."

"Because a madman walked into a building with the intent to hurt people. To kill people. And he would've hurt and killed even more if it wasn't for you."

He tried to ease his hand away from hers but she wouldn't let him.

"A kid will still be growing up never knowing her own father."

"And that's a tragedy. But she won't blame you for it. She'll blame the man who walked into her father's offices with weapons of death in his hands."

It was plain to see Joe wasn't convinced. That he carried more than just physical scars from that particular attack.

Laura held on to his hand tighter. All law enforcement workers were heroes in her opinion, but for some reason she hadn't really included Joe in that group.

Why?

Because she'd convinced herself that his money, his charm and his charisma somehow kept him sheltered, separated from the most painful aspects of his job.

She realized with no small sense of shame that her line of thinking was the same reason Joe felt like he wasn't truly part of the Omega team. Because people thought his job as hostage negotiator was just a hobby for him. That he was doing it as some sort of charity work he could walk away from at any time.

That he wasn't invested.

Everything about the conversation they'd just had—from the words he'd said to the way he'd held himself as he'd said them—told her otherwise.

Joe was every bit as much of a hero as other law enforcement personnel. Just because he didn't need the money they paid him didn't make him any less of one. Although he'd never admit it, probably even to himself, it hurt Joe to think that other people assumed he didn't care as much as they did.

Joe did.

Laura was still pondering the man she realized she didn't really know, still holding his hand tightly in her lap when they pulled up to the address Joe's contact had provided.

"What do we do now?" She turned to look

at the apartment complex where the Goldman brothers were staying.

"It's early on a Saturday morning. I'm going to assume neither of the Goldmans is leaving for a job anytime soon. So I'm going in there and you're staying out here."

She watched as he reached into the glove compartment of the car and pulled out two guns.

"I thought you had to turn in your gun at Omega when you gave Steve your badge."

Joe gave an innocent shrug then winked at her. "I had to turn in my official weapon, but it certainly wasn't my only weapon. These are both Glock 42s. Are you familiar with handguns?"

"I've been to the shooting range a few times, but not with this particular pistol."

Joe showed her the basics and left one of them with her.

"I don't like leaving you here alone, but I like even less the thought of taking you in there with

Max and Melvin. Just stay here and keep your eyes open for any trouble."

"Like what?"

"Like the police, who will gladly arrest both me and them and sort it out later."

Laura grimaced. She couldn't pull a gun on the police and expect it to end well for anyone.

Joe took out his phone and showed her the info his guy Deacon had sent. It was surprisingly thorough given the man had only had an hour to put it together. Pictures of Max and Melvin without their masks—looking remarkably like Ricky and Bobby in the bank, a photo of their apartment, stats on their life—unemployed, unmarried, both in their 20s, neither with a college education.

"Do you think they're just going to confess?"

"No. But we're not dealing with rocket scientists here. All I need to do is get them to let it slip that they know anything about any of the women and then we can start hunting down details in earnest."

"Joe, questioning people is what I do for a living. I'm a lawyer. Let me come in with you."

Joe stared at her for a long time.

"You know I'm right. Having two of us there is much better than just one."

He grimaced, not liking it but having to accept the truth of her statement. "Fine. But I'm going in there first. Once I have them secured then I will call you and you can come up. You don't come up without a message from me, no matter what. Got it?"

Laura rolled her eyes. "Yeah, got it. Little woman will just sit in the car waiting for the big strong man to face all the danger."

Joe reached over and grabbed her chin, pulling her to him. He gave her a hard kiss, almost bruising in its intensity.

"I'm not taking any chances with your life. You're too valuable to me. Wait for my message."

He was out of the door before she'd even caught her breath.

WHAT THE HELL was he doing? Joe walked silently up the stairs to the second floor apartment the Goldman brothers lived in. Laura had been right in the cabin when she'd suggested he call in some Omega backup.

Going in here alone seemed like a fine plan when it had just been him. But now that he was bringing in Laura, having more good guys in the room seemed like a much better plan.

But his arguments still applied. He couldn't drag his colleagues into this. Or, more honestly, couldn't trust they would choose to take his word over what seemed like pretty damning evidence.

Either way, it was too late now. Joe needed answers from the Goldman brothers and he needed them directly.

He knocked on the door, keeping his face averted in case they were smart enough to use the peephole in their door.

"Doughnut delivery. We have your order ready."

Joe didn't know of any places that delivered

doughnuts, but it seemed less suspicious than pizza this early in the morning. All he needed was for them to open the door just the slightest bit.

He pulled his gun out from where he'd tucked it into the waistband of his jeans.

The door cracked open. "Look, we didn't order no—"

Joe flew into the door with his uninjured shoulder, sending it slamming open and the man—it looked like Melvin by his picture and arm in a sling—flying back to the ground. Joe immediately trained his weapon on him.

"Where's your brother?" Joe asked, looking around the small place without taking his gun off Melvin.

"You!"

"Yeah, me. You guys should've finished the job when you had the chance." He used his foot to push the door back.

"How did you find us?"

"Believe it or not, Einstein, finding out details about other people is not difficult in this day and age." Particularly when you had a Deacon Crandall on your side. "Especially when you know what you're looking for. Where's Max?"

Melvin looked back and forth from one bedroom to the other.

He cocked his head to the side. "He's sleeping."

Joe eased his way toward the room Melvin gestured to and opened the door.

There was no one in the bed, sleeping or otherwise.

He caught Melvin's grin out of the corner of his eye and realized he'd made a mistake underestimating the man. Joe wasn't going to be able to stop whoever he could feel flying toward him.

Chapter Fifteen

Joe's gun slid out of his hand as Max tackled him. He must've come through the front door. Joe would've seen him come out either of the bedrooms.

He grunted as Max's fist found his face and realized Melvin would soon have Joe's gun. Things were getting out of hand quickly and the only saving grace was that Laura waited safely in the car.

"If you touch that weapon, I'm going to be forced to shoot you."

Maybe Laura wasn't safely in the car.

"And you." She turned her Glock toward Max and Joe. "Get off of him. Joe, are you alright?"

Joe pushed Max to the side and onto the floor by his brother. He picked up his own weapon.

"You suck at following directions, you know that? What part of 'stay in the car until you hear from me' didn't you understand?"

Laura rolled her eyes. "The part where I saw Max arrive after you and thought maybe I should come in and see if you needed help. Which it looks like you did."

She kept her gun trained at the Goldman brothers and damn if that wasn't one of the sexiest things he'd ever seen. He wrapped an arm around her waist and kissed her forehead.

"Thanks."

She smiled. "No problem."

Joe shut and locked the front door and checked the rest of the rooms to make sure there wouldn't be any more surprises. He found some plastic zip-ties and used them to restrain Max's arms behind his back. He swore Melvin would get the same treatment also, regardless of his broken wrist, if he gave them any problems.

"You going to arrest us like you did Michael and Mitchell?"

Joe shook his head. "Your brothers took sixteen people hostage in a bank. Hurt two of them. They deserved whatever they got. But I wasn't the one who arrested them."

"That's not what they said," Mitchell muttered.

"I was the one in there making sure the SWAT team didn't kill them outright. So the next time your brothers want to talk trash about me, you remind them that I am the reason they aren't sitting in the morgue right now, rather than in a cell."

Max and Melvin glanced at each other. Evidently the facts Joe provided didn't jibe with what their brothers had told them.

"But no, I don't plan to arrest you." Mostly because Joe was wanted by the law himself, although he wouldn't be telling them that. "I just need answers to some questions."

"You were trying to kidnap me in the parking garage on Thursday," Laura interjected. "Why? To kill me like the rest and frame Joe for it?"

"What?" Mitchell's eyes flew to her. "No. We weren't going to kill you. We were just going to hold you hostage until they let our brothers out."

Laura pointed at Melvin. "You had a knife."

The man shrugged. "I always have a knife. You never know when you're going to need it. But I wasn't planning to kill you with it." He turned to Joe. "I wasn't even planning to kill you with it. I just got a little carried away in the moment."

"What about Olivia? Or Jessica or Sarah? Did you kill them with your knife?"

Melvin looked over at his brother then back at Joe. His face had lost all color. "Dude. I swear I didn't kill nobody. Not with a knife, not with anything. I don't even know who you're talking about."

Joe grabbed Melvin by the shirt. "I think you do know what I'm talking about. I think you killed those three women because you were mad at me for bringing down your brothers, and you were planning to kill Laura, too."

Melvin was sweating now. "No. I swear, man. I have no idea who those other girls are. We were just taking her—" he gestured to Laura "—to get the police to let Mitchell and Michael go."

Joe resisted the urge to ram his fist into the other man's face. He wasn't a violent man by nature, but the thought of his exes' pointless deaths filled him with rage. A rage that had nothing on what he felt about Laura being their next victim.

It was Laura who brought him back, touching him on the arm. She kept her back to the Goldman brothers and leaned her face close to his. "Look at them. I think they might be telling the truth. Let me ask them some questions."

He didn't want to. He just wanted to pound on them until their blood covered his hands.

Laura reached up and touched his jaw. "Joe, you're not in this alone. Trust me to help you with this."

Joe nodded and released Melvin, who fell back, still sweating.

Laura turned to them.

"You boys been watching the news over the last week?"

"Nah. Our cable got cut off since we didn't pay the bill," Melvin said.

"You heard anything about three women in the greater Denver/Colorado Springs area being murdered over the last few days?"

Both men shook their heads. "No. We didn't know nothing about that," Max told her. "We've been busy trying to figure out how to get our brothers out of jail."

"And that's why you came after me."

The brothers looked at each other then nodded.

But they were hiding something. Joe wanted to stop Laura, demand the men tell them what it was they were hiding. But Laura touched his arm so Joe kept quiet. She'd asked him to trust her.

A team meant trust on both sides.

"Tell me your plan once you had me," Laura demanded.

Melvin sat up a little straighter, obviously happy they weren't accusing him of murder anymore. "We were going to put a call in to the police telling them we had a hostage. Demand that Joe Matarazzo meet with us. Once he saw it was you we had hostage he would do whatever it took to get our brothers out. Since they were innocent."

Joe barely restrained from rolling his eyes.

Laura continued questioning. "Did your brothers tell you how much Joe cared about me from when they saw us in the bank together?"

Max and Melvin looked at each other again. "Not exactly," Max responded.

Laura nodded. "That's what I thought. Because Joe and I didn't even talk to each other in front of your brothers. So there was no way they would've known he cared for me any more than he cared for anyone else. Who told you that, Max?" She turned and looked at the other brother. "You didn't come up with the plan to kidnap me yourself, right, Melvin? You boys didn't really want to hurt me. You're not kidnappers. You're not murderers. Who gave you the idea?"

Joe just sat back and watched Laura work. He had no doubt she was this formidable in the courtroom also. Melvin and Max had no chance against her.

"Some lady," Max blubbered. "She came up to us on Wednesday. Said she had seen the whole bank thing on Friday and had a way we could get our brothers out of jail."

"Yeah, like you said, we didn't want to hurt anybody," Melvin chimed in. "We just wanted to help them. She told us where you worked. Where you would be coming out and when. Told us that Joe would do anything for you, even get our brothers out of jail."

Joe stepped up and grabbed Max's shirt. "Who? Who told you all this?"

"We don't know her name. I swear."

Melvin nodded. "She knew everything about you, man. Loved talking about you and all the details she knew. All the women you dated and all the money you had. Talked about some burn scars."

"She was kind of scary." Max's voice lowered. "Wild look in her eyes, you know? Said you deserved to be punished." Max looked at Joe. "Said you deserved to burn."

"But she said first you would help us get our brothers out. If we took Laura and held her ransom, you would get our brothers out."

"More likely she would've killed all three of us and framed Joe for the murder." Laura dropped her gun to her side.

Both men's eyes bugged out.

"What did she look like?" Joe asked.

"Long black hair," Max said. "Really pretty."

"Yeah, sort of tall for a woman. Maybe five foot nine. Curvy. Nice rack."

Trust these two idiots to remember her breast measurements.

"How old was she?" Joe demanded, trying to think of women from his past who fit the description.

Max shrugged. "I don't know. Our age. Mid-twenties."

"Had her hair pulled back in a tight bun."

"Joe." Laura pulled him closer to her so the brothers couldn't hear. "I know who they're talking about."

"Who?"

"I don't know her name, but she was at the

garage the day they tried to grab me. I saw her. She was sort of staring at me. I thought she had just forgotten where her car was parked. But now I know she was definitely watching."

"Do you remember what she looks like? Do you think you could identify her again?"

"Absolutely."

It was a start. The Goldman brothers weren't the ones trying to frame Joe. But at least they now had something on the person who was.

They just had to find her.

Chapter Sixteen

They went back to Laura's house in Fountain, rather than the cabin. It was time to stop running, stop hiding. Joe would always have fond memories of the cabin, but the next time he took Laura there, it wouldn't be to escape police trying to arrest him.

Her house was a risk since the cops were still looking for him, but Joe was going to stay and fight.

And he'd called in for reinforcements. Laura was right—he'd be stupid to try to fight this battle alone. Upon leaving Max and Melvin's apartment, Joe had called Steve. He'd let Steve know what the Goldman brothers had told him: their suspect was a woman.

And she seemed to know a great deal about Joe's professional and private life.

The first thing they needed to do was search through any footage they had of crowds surrounding Joe's hostage cases. Omega routinely recorded the crowds that gathered at cases and investigations. Often the perpetrator couldn't resist coming back to inspect his or her handiwork.

Joe knew that woman was in the footage somewhere. But as evidenced by the number of case files they'd had to steal, Joe had worked on dozens of hostage cases in his career. It was going to take a long time to go through that footage.

Time they didn't have.

Steve agreed to send someone to pick up the Goldman brothers, keeping them out of the hands of the Colorado Springs PD for a little while, and to send someone with the digitized footage to Laura's house.

At least they didn't have to break into Omega to get the footage. Joe hadn't liked asking for anything, but Steve hadn't even hesitated when Joe made his request.

It was sort of a weird feeling, trusting someone to help him.

Laura was taking a shower and changing into her own clothes when the doorbell rang. Joe checked to make sure it wasn't the police and was surprised to find that instead of some low-level courier Joe had been expecting from Omega, it was Jon Hatton.

Joe opened the door. "Hey, wasn't expecting you."

"I have some footage Steve insisted I bring over. Not only am I one of Omega's top profilers and crisis management experts, I am now a pack mule."

Sherry Mitchell, Jon's fiancée and forensic artist, stepped out from behind him. "Don't listen to his lies, Joe. He volunteered. Plus I have doughnuts."

Joe let them through and introduced them both to Laura when she came down from her shower. Within just a few minutes Joe and Jon were getting the footage set up on multiple computers as Sherry worked with Laura to create a drawing of the woman she'd seen in the parking lot.

Sherry labored patiently with Laura for the next two hours, asking her questions and helping her remember seeing details about the woman. She was truly a gifted forensic artist.

"My gal is something else, isn't she?" Jon asked.

"Unbelievably talented." Joe couldn't doubt it.

Jon smiled. "It's nice to see Sherry working with someone who isn't traumatized. Normally she works with rape or battery victims. Kidnappings. It's not easy for her." He walked over and kissed her on the head. Sherry just smiled up at him and kept working.

Finally they had a drawing. A clear image of a woman.

"That's definitely the lady I saw in the parking garage." Laura handed the picture to Joe. "Do you recognize her?"

She didn't look familiar at all. "She's definitely not someone I've ever dated." He rolled his eyes at Jon. "Despite what you and the rest of the gang think, I do actually remember the people I've gone out with. I would remember this woman's face if I knew her."

Jon took the picture. "I'm going to send this to Steve, see if the Goldman brothers recognize her." He snapped a picture with his phone.

"Alright. We've got a face. Let's start studying footage at crime scenes I've been involved with." Too bad facial recognition software wouldn't work from a drawing. Plus, if the woman wasn't in their database it wouldn't help anyway.

"It's going to be slow going with all the cases," Jon pointed out.

"Then we better get started."

They each had a computer or laptop and split the cases. Then began the grueling process of pausing each video and comparing the drawing to the people in the crowds. Crowds that were sometimes hundreds of people thick.

"Steve just texted me back. Confirmed that is the woman who approached the Goldman brothers."

At least they knew they were looking for the right person. Even if it was going to take forever to find her.

The doorbell rang again and Laura's eyes flew to Joe's. They both worried it was the police.

But it wasn't. More of Joe's Omega colleagues had arrived. SWAT members Derek Waterman, Lillian Muir and Liam Goetz, Derek's wife Molly who worked at the Omega lab, even Brandon Han and Andrea Gordon, who had helped him at the first crime scene when Sarah had been found.

They were all here, on their day off, laptops in hand.

"Heard you needed more eyes." Derek slapped him on the back on his way in.

"Yes, Joe, we want to help." Molly waddled through. "Especially when this big buffoon won't let me do almost anything else. I'm pregnant, not terminally ill." She smacked Derek on the arm.

Never had Joe expected to see his colleagues here. Especially not en masse. Not to help him.

"You guys, I…" Joe shrugged not sure how to even finish the sentence.

Andrea, who he had gotten to know a little better last month when they'd watched over Brandon Han in the hospital smiled at him. "Joe, we want to help. All of us."

Of everyone here, Andrea probably most understood how Joe felt. Until recently she'd kept herself, and the fact that she used to be a stripper, far away from all her colleagues, afraid to ever make attachments.

Joe wasn't ashamed of his past, but he'd sort of done the same thing: kept himself apart, thinking they didn't really include him in their inner circle.

Although with Laura's house almost full to overflowing with people here to help him—here because they wanted to be, not because it was part of a case or an order from Steve—he could no longer use that reasoning.

He was part of the team.

As everyone settled in at a computer, Jon divvying up the cases, Laura made her way over to Joe. He could see the smile she tried to keep tamped down.

"You going to say I told you so?" he asked as she sat next to him, laptop in hand.

"I would never stoop so low." She grinned. "But maybe nanny-nanny-boo-boo."

Joe lowered his voice so no one else could hear. "I can't believe they're all here."

"You'd do the same for any of them, right? If they were in danger and needed your help? Even if it was off-the-record and might get you in trouble?"

"Sure."

"Same thing. You're part of the team, Matarazzo. Money, no money. Gossip sites or not. They have your back. Just like you would have theirs."

Joe didn't tend to be at a loss for words very often, but looking around the room, watching his friends stare at screens, doughnuts in most of their hands, he was.

"I don't know what to say to them."

Laura reached over and cupped his cheeks. "You don't have to say anything. That's the great thing about family. They just do what needs to be done, no words necessary."

Joe had grown up with a lot of money, a lot of

privilege, trips, gadgets…but he'd never really had family. The best boarding schools money could buy, but no one close.

"Family." The word seemed awkward on his tongue.

"Family isn't always blood, and blood isn't always family." She smiled. "Now get to work."

Joe looked back down at his screen realizing Laura was right. These people were his family. In every way that counted.

"I've got her." Liam Goetz's voice called out.

"Are you sure?" Joe asked.

Liam grinned. "One hundred percent. Check her out." The laptop got passed around. No one could doubt that was the woman Laura had described and Sherry had drawn.

"You're spooky good," Laura said to Sherry, who just shrugged.

"What about me?" Liam said. "I found her. Isn't anyone going to tell me how awesome I am?"

Somebody threw a pillow at him.

"What case is that?" Jon asked.

Liam put the pillow behind his back. "Jewelry store hostage situation in Palm Springs. Ten months ago."

Everyone looked at Joe. He shrugged. "I remember it, but there wasn't much out of the ordinary. No casualties. Hostage-takers stepped down without the use of force."

"Okay, let's branch out from that case, see if we can find her," Jon said. "I'm going to send the picture to Omega, see if she blips on any of our facial recognition software. Maybe we'll get lucky."

Laura began looking through the case file for the jewelry store while everyone began searching footage with a renewed sense of purpose.

"You're right," Laura agreed after reading through the file. "I don't see anything in this case that would make someone angry at you."

"I've got her again," Lillian said a few minutes

later. "Six months ago. She's in the crowd when that guy was threatening to blow himself up at the home improvement store. I remember that."

SWAT had to take the guy out. Joe couldn't help him. That had been clear early on.

"Yep, I've got her in Austin last month," Derek said. "Right at the very front of the crowd."

"Wow. Looks like Joe has got himself a stalker." Liam smirked. "Some guys have all the luck."

"I'm afraid Liam's right, Joe," Derek's wife, Molly, cut in before Joe could make a sarcastic comment to Liam. "I have her in the crowd at last weekend's bank heist."

Joe looked over at Laura. Her expression was as worried as he knew his had to be. This woman had been following him for months.

"Okay." Jon took charge. "Everybody get a screen shot of when you have her, as well as the date and location. We need to find out when she first started showing up."

Laura ordered pizzas for lunch as they continued to look. The woman was everywhere. She had been at every case Joe had worked on for at least the past year. Had traveled all over the country to watch him.

Downright scary.

"Okay, I don't have her," Brandon Han said. "I'm one hundred percent positive she's not in this crowd."

Nobody asked to double-check Brandon. The man was a certifiable genius. If he said the mystery woman wasn't in the crowd, then she wasn't.

"Okay," Joe said. "Let's check the case immediately before that. Maybe she was sick that day or something."

They didn't find her on the footage of the previous case either. Or the one before that.

"It looks like she first made an appearance at the Castlehill Offices case," Lillian said, voice grim. "I've got her there."

Silence fell over the room.

"Which case is that?" Laura asked, coming to stand by Joe.

He wrapped an arm around her. "The one we were talking about this morning. Where I lost four hostages to the guy with the grenade."

"Joe, none of us knew that guy had such a death wish and need for revenge," Lillian said. "Or that he had the grenade. I was watching through my rifle sights from the other building and didn't see it."

Derek stood. "Yeah, Joe. We were all there, and have all reviewed the footage. There was no way you could've known. Sometimes people are just crazy."

Joe shrugged. Regardless of whether the guy was crazy or not, four people had died.

"Joe," Andrea's soft voice cut in. She didn't say much, didn't waste words, so when she did talk, everyone listened. "Look at these pictures of the woman."

Andrea brought her laptop over to stand with

Joe and Laura. "Look at her at the Castlehill Offices. She's distraught, terrified." She flicked the screen to show other pictures from other crime scenes. "Now look at her as time progresses. She's becoming filled with rage. Resolve."

Andrea had a wonderful gift as a behavioral analyst. Her ability to read people's nonverbal communication and emotion was uncanny.

"On cases where you were successful and no one was hurt she's most angry. On cases where SWAT had to be used, she's less so," Andrea continued. "Regardless, she is connected to someone—probably one of the victims who died—at Castlehill. I can almost guarantee that."

Joe had thought he was on good terms with the victims' families—as good as someone who had caused the death of their loved ones could be. But evidently he'd been wrong. It was time to talk to the families again. See if any of them knew this woman.

SHE HAD WATCHED *them all come in this morn-ing, and watched them all leave a few at a time.*

She thought of setting a fire while they all gathered inside. Of barring the doors so no one could escape. But she didn't have what she needed in her van.

She pulled at her hair and rocked back and forth. She'd missed a perfect opportunity be-cause she was unprepared.

But no. That plan would've killed innocent people. People who had no part in Tyler's death.

She had to stay focused. Punish only Joe and anyone he loved or who loved him. These people he worked with did not love him. He kept him-self separate from them almost always.

She'd been surprised to see them here at all.

She counted them as they left to make sure they were all gone. Then watched, rage boiling through her veins as Joe left hand in hand with the lawyer woman, Laura.

Why should Joe Matarazzo find love when he'd killed her Tyler?

Tyler had loved her. Would've eventually made a life with her.

She forced herself to remain calm until Joe and the woman were far away, then made her way to the house.

Inside the house.

All she needed now was patience. That she had.

Joe Matarazzo would burn like Tyler did. And the woman would burn with him.

Chapter Seventeen

"I talked to all the families after the victims died, but have remained closest with Summer Worrall," Joe said as they drove toward the woman's house.

Laura didn't know exactly what her feelings were on the fact that Joe had remained close with the young widow of one of the men who had been killed under his watch.

She knew even less when Summer opened the door and invited them in.

The woman was beautiful. Slender, despite having just had a baby in the last few months, petite with auburn hair and big green eyes. She had a fragile, tragic air about her. It made Laura want to take the woman in her arms.

She could imagine that Joe felt the exact same way.

Summer took Joe in her arms instead.

"Joe! What are you doing here?" She hugged him hard. Joe looked over at Laura with an apologetic smile as he hugged Summer back.

As if Laura would begrudge him hugging someone who had gone through so much tragedy.

Laura just wished the woman wasn't quite so *beautifully* tragic. Shouldn't someone with a newborn look frazzled and sleep-deprived?

"Please, both of you, come in." She turned to Laura. "I'm Summer Worrall."

"I'm Laura Birchwood, Joe's lawyer."

"She's my girlfriend, too, Summer."

Laura expected a laugh or raised eyebrow at that announcement, but the other woman just grinned. "Good. He needs someone to keep him in line." She opened the door wider so they could come in.

"How's Chloe?" Joe asked, walking toward the living room. He'd obviously been here before.

"She's beautiful. Sleeps like an angel, thank God. It makes a huge difference that I can stay home. Joe. Again, I wanted to say thank—"

Joe put a finger over the woman's lips. "You've already said it multiple times. No need to say it again. It's no trouble."

Laura almost felt like she was intruding on an intimate moment. Joe and Summer obviously knew each other and had a rapport that needed more than what a single "I'm sorry your husband was killed" visit would provide. There didn't seem to be anything romantic between the two of them, but definitely a closeness.

But Joe grabbed Laura's hand as he sat down on the sofa across from Summer, so Laura let it all go.

"We're here on business, Summer," Joe said.

The other woman looked a little surprised. Obviously Joe didn't usually come over to her house for business.

"Does it have to do with your ex-girlfriends who died?"

"Yes." Joe nodded. "But I didn't have anything to do with their deaths."

Summer stared at him as if he had lost his mind. "It never occurred to me that you'd had anything to do with it."

Anybody who knew Joe would never think he had anything to do with it. Laura had been trying to tell him that all week.

Joe brought out his phone and pulled up a picture of the woman from the crime scenes. He showed it to Summer.

"Do you know who this woman is?"

She startled them both by flying out of her chair and snatching the phone out of Joe's hand. Tears immediately began streaming down her face.

Laura and Joe both stood at the sudden movement. Laura was closest to the woman and put an arm around her. "Are you okay? What's wrong?"

"Where did you get that picture?"

"She's a woman who has been hanging around a lot of crime scenes. Particularly hostage situations where I've been involved."

Summer looked at Laura then at Joe. "You have to stay away from her. She's dangerous. Crazy."

"Do you know who she is?" Laura asked. Summer was visibly shaking. Laura led her to the sofa so she could sit down.

"Her name is Bailey Heath." Summer looked at the picture again. "She's emotionally unstable."

"Have you met her, Summer?" Joe asked. He was probably thinking along the same lines as Laura was: Summer and her daughter might need protection from this woman.

"Not recently. Tyler and I had a restraining order against her before he died."

"Why?"

"Tyler and Bailey worked together at Castle-hill for a few months. She became obsessed with him. He talked to their bosses and they transferred her to another building after looking into it."

Laura squeezed her hand. "But that didn't keep her away?"

Summer shook her head. "Then she just started showing up at the house. She would follow me around and tell me that Tyler loved her and would be leaving me soon."

"Do you think there was any truth at all to the statements?" Joe asked gently.

"No. None. I trusted him completely." Her eyes filled with tears again. "Tyler and I spent hours talking about what he might have done that gave her any impression he was interested at all, much less intending to break up his marriage for her. He hated that he had somehow allowed her into our lives."

Summer took a shuddery breath. "She's unbalanced. Would sit outside our house and watch it for days on end. That's when we got a restraining order."

Laura rubbed her back. "Definitely the right thing to do."

"You can tell she's sort of crazy after just talking to her for a few minutes. She fully believes whatever fantasy world she's living in is actual reality. There's no way to convince her otherwise."

"Has she contacted you at all since Tyler's death?"

"No. Thank God. Somebody told me she was at Tyler's funeral, but I didn't see her. And I had too much to worry about to deal with her then."

Laura's eyes met Joe's. At least it seemed that Summer and Samantha weren't on Bailey's hit list.

"Why are you asking about her?"

Joe's brows knitted. "We think she might be

involved with killing my ex-girlfriends. It seems like she's got an axe to grind against me."

"She was so obsessed with Tyler," Summer whispered. "Maybe she blames you for his death. The one-year anniversary of his death was on Sunday you know."

Joe glanced up sharply. "That's when the first woman was killed."

"That could've been what triggered her. The fact that it had been a year." Laura frowned. Bailey Heath obviously was holding on to her delusions pretty tightly.

Joe came over to crouch by Summer. "I'm sorry that I didn't come by. I should have remembered."

Summer patted him on the cheek. "Joe, Tyler's death was not your fault. I have never for one moment of one day blamed you for him dying. You have to stop blaming yourself. His death was a tragedy, but not *your* tragedy."

Joe nodded and stood. Obviously this wasn't

a new topic of conversation between he and Summer.

"Now that we know who the woman in the picture is we've got to find her. Stop her before she strikes again."

Laura nodded. Summer had never blamed Joe for Tyler's death, but there was a psycho out there who did.

"WHAT WAS SUMMER about to thank you for at her house when you stopped her?"

They were on their way back to Laura's house. Joe had already put in a call to Omega. Steve had issued an APB to try to find Bailey Heath. Brandon Han was working up a profile on her based on what information they could find. Andrea Gordon was studying the footage to try to read any nonverbals she could.

The team was working overtime to try to clear Joe's name. Laura knew he appreciated it. If nothing good came of this entire situation, at least Joe would know his friends truly considered him part of the Omega family.

"No big deal. I found Summer a job."

"I'm sure there's more to it than that."

Joe rolled his eyes. "Fine. I created a job for her. She manages social media for some of the Matarazzo holdings."

"But it allows her to work at home. So she can be with baby Chloe."

He gave a self-deprecating laugh. "I tried to just give her money outright, but she wouldn't take it."

"She doesn't blame you. She would've taken the money if she blamed you."

He shrugged. "I still want to help out whatever way I can. I started a college fund for Chloe. She'll be able to go wherever she wants to go."

"The best thing we can do for both of them right now is get Bailey Heath behind bars."

"Absolutely."

He pulled up to a side road close to her house

and parked. They weren't parking in her driveway in case the police came by still looking for Joe.

Laura opened the door to get out of the car but he stopped her, grabbing her arm.

"What's wrong?"

"That van over there. Do you know it? Does it belong to any of your neighbors?"

A white cargo van, pretty nondescript. "I don't think so. Somebody could be having some work done or something."

"It was parked there when everyone got here this morning. Still there ten hours later. A long time for a work van to be parked in a residential neighborhood, especially on a Saturday."

They got out of the car and Joe led them down the sidewalk away from both her house and the van. "We'll walk around the block and circle back to it."

Laura felt Joe's arm snake around her waist. She

couldn't help but lean in to him. "What you're doing for Summer is admirable, you know."

He shrugged. "The least I could do."

He kept her tugged to his side, keeping their stride casual, until they came up on the van.

"Stand to the side while I announce myself as federal law enforcement. If anything goes bad, just get out of the way, okay?" He kissed the side of her head.

"Are you expecting anything to go wrong?"

"One thing I've learned with my years at Omega is to expect anything."

Once they were on the rear side of the van he turned to her, taking his gun from his holster. He banged on the back door. "This is federal law enforcement. If anyone is in there, I need you to open the door."

Nothing happened. Joe looked over at her, without lowering his weapon. "If it's unlocked, you pull the door open and keep out of the way."

"Be careful."

He motioned a countdown with his finger and Laura pulled the handle. Finding it unlocked, she pulled the back door wide-open, stepping to the side as she did so.

In just a few moments, Joe replaced his weapon in the holster under his jacket. "It's clear. Really is a work van. Go figure."

She peeked around the door. Sure enough some paint cans and cloths lay on the floor of the van, some tools and other items strewn about.

Nothing suspicious.

They closed the door and Joe put his forehead against hers. "I'm paranoid. I'm sorry."

"Hey, I'm a lawyer. I'm all about the 'rather safe than sorry' theory. Especially when the person we're looking for has a history of sitting outside of someone's house and watching."

Joe pulled her close again and they crossed the street to her house. She handed him the key to her door. "You know, I think it's safer for you if I stay at your house until we find Bailey Heath."

He slid her jacket off her shoulders and Laura turned to look at him, smiling. "Oh yeah? And is some psychopath stalker the only reason you're interested in staying here?"

He hung her jacket on the back of a dining room chair and soon his followed suit. He turned his gaze on her. It could be called nothing less than predatory.

Everything inside her heated at the look in his eyes.

"Are you saying you might be interested in something other than me being your body-guard?" He took a step closer.

"I'm pretty sure there's something I'd like you to do with my body, but guard isn't what I had in mind." She gripped the waistband of his jeans and pulled him closer. She took a step back until her spine was fully up against the door.

He was everything she should run from. He was everything she craved.

All she knew was if he was here, she wasn't

going to waste a chance to enjoy him again. Enjoy *them* again.

She licked her lips.

He groaned and pushed his body flush against hers. "If you don't stop looking at me like that, we're not even going to make it up to the bedroom."

"Maybe I don't want to make it to the bedroom."

She felt his lips work their way up her throat to her lips. Not a gentle, searching kiss.

Hot. Demanding.

The way it had always been with them.

As Joe slipped off his shirt she saw the scar on the side of his neck more clearly now that she knew what it was from.

She had almost lost him that day and she'd never even known. The thought caused her to pull him closer, even more desperate not to have space between them. He obliged, cupping her face and licking deep into her mouth.

They both moaned and tore at the rest of the clothes between them.

Somewhere in the back of Laura's mind she knew she was letting herself fall too hard. Letting Joe mean too much to her again. The price she would pay when he finally walked away again would be too high.

But when his lips worked their way to her ear then lowered to her throat she pushed the voice of reason down where it couldn't be heard.

And let the flames engulf her.

Chapter Eighteen

Joe studied Laura as she slept beside him. It was late on Sunday morning. They'd spent the entire night laughing and talking and making love.

His heart broke at the pointless deaths of those women from his past, but part of him was grateful it had thrown Laura back into his life so completely.

She wouldn't be in this bed with him otherwise—he knew that for sure. Laura's wariness had flashed in her eyes last night when she thought he wouldn't see it. Not when they were making love—he knew for certain her guard remained down then—but other times.

Like when she had mentioned a colleague's white-water rafting trip and he'd stated they should go together this summer. She'd smiled, then smoothly changed the subject.

Laura wasn't making any future plans with him.

At first he thought it was because she didn't want to spend time with him in the future. But gradually he'd come to realize that she was waiting for him to change his mind again.

Bracing herself for the impact.

Joe would give every dime he had if he could go back and change the stupid, panicked words he'd said that night six years ago.

But all he could do was keep Laura as close to him as possible. Love her every single day until it saturated every thought she had.

Love used to be a word that scared Joe. Not anymore. Not when it had to do with Laura.

"Hey," she whispered, her eyes opening a little. "What are you growling about over there?"

He hooked an arm over her hip. "No growling. Just determination."

To have her. With him. For the rest of both their lives.

"To catch Bailey Heath?"

The temptation to tell her his complete thoughts almost overwhelmed him. Only the knowledge that she couldn't accept it, wouldn't believe him if he started declaring his true feelings for her, stopped him.

"Yeah. There's been no word on her yet."

"How long does Steve think it will take to find her?"

"She's got the full weight of Omega's resources on her shoulders. That's a lot. They've fed her image into the facial recognition program. That thing is pretty damn scary. If she drives past a traffic light, uses an ATM, walks past any security camera that uplinks to a mobile server, she'll get tagged."

"Good. She needs to be caught."

He reached over and kissed her. "She will be, don't worry. Not many people can hide from Omega for long. Particularly someone with no covert training."

"Speaking of not hiding anymore, I think you ought to consider turning yourself in to the police."

"Won't they arrest me?"

"I don't think so with the new evidence that has come to light. We'll show them what we have on Bailey Heath. The Goldman brothers are in custody and can attest to her hatred for you and that she had suggested my kidnapping. Plus, we'll have Steve call and back up everything you're saying."

A couple of days ago Joe would've been loath to ask Steve to do even that, but this situation had changed everything.

"I can't be in a cell. Not right now, not with her still out there. I won't leave you unprotected." He pulled her over to lie against his chest.

"Why don't we call Brandon Han and get his opinion? He's a great lawyer and I think he'll agree with me. Plus, walking into the station of your own accord, rather than being picked up, goes a long way toward proving you have nothing to hide."

"Alright, I'll call Brandon." The other man might be on a different case—along with being licensed to practice law, he was also one of the best profilers in Omega—but he would come if he could.

"We just need everybody in law enforcement looking for her. Not wasting any time or resources looking for you."

He reached in and kissed her. "I agree. And if both you and Brandon feel confident that they're not going to throw me in jail then I'll go."

"Even if they do, we could expedite a bond hearing and get you out on bail by tomorrow."

Joe would have to think about whether he was willing to risk leaving Laura even for a night.

He would have to trust his friends at Omega to keep her safe.

Could he do that?

He ran a hand down Laura's cheek. He realized that he could do it. He could trust them. Trust her. Not that he'd have a good night's sleep being apart from her, but he could trust the team to guard Laura if it became a necessity.

Because what was important to Joe was important to them.

It was nice to know someone had his back. And that it had nothing to do with his money. His team wanted nothing in return.

She cupped his hand where it rested against her cheek. "Okay, as much as I'd love to lie naked in bed with you all day, that's not going to get your name cleared with the police."

She slipped out of bed and Joe leaned back against the pillows with his arms linked behind his head enjoying the view as Laura put on yoga pants and a T-shirt. "Actually, I'm pretty sure if you showed up at the precinct naked they would give you anything you wanted."

She smiled at him and he literally felt his breath being taken away. Laura might never be a beauty in the classic sense but damn if she wasn't the most gorgeous thing he'd ever seen.

"Maybe I'll try that at my next court case."

"I'll be sure to clear my calendar." And clear the courtroom so he'd be the only one able to lay eyes on a naked Laura. "I'm going to take a shower."

"I'll get coffee and breakfast going then we can call Brandon."

She bent to tie on a pair of sneakers and he patted her bottom on his way to the bathroom. The temptation to do more, to drag her back to bed and remove the clothes she'd just put on, almost overwhelmed him. But she was right, they needed to go to the police and get his name cleared.

Joe turned the shower on and stepped in before the water could even turn warm. The cold helped get his raging body under control and Joe didn't fight it, despite preferring to handle it a much more pleasurable way.

He wanted his name cleared. Wanted the women from his past—and his much more important present—to be safe. He wanted this behind him so he could court Laura properly the way he desired. The way she deserved.

The water turned warmer and Joe quickly finished his shower. Now that he had a plan in place he didn't want to waste any time putting it into action. After toweling off and getting dressed he grabbed his phone off the bathroom counter and put in a call to Brandon.

"Hey, Joe, how are you hanging in there?" Brandon answered by way of greeting. "Any news on Bailey Heath?"

"Nothing that I've heard so far."

"It won't take long with all of Omega's resources utilized in the hunt."

"That's my hope. Laura thinks I should voluntarily submit myself to the Colorado Springs PD." Joe explained what he and Laura had discussed. "She wanted to know if you could come over to review anything she might be missing."

"Well, I'm sort of in the middle of something." Joe heard Brandon whisper something to someone at his house.

Of course. It was Sunday morning. Brandon would be with Andrea.

"Brandon, I understand. Seriously, man—"

Another conversation Joe couldn't quite hear.

"Never mind. We'll be there in thirty minutes. Andrea says we'll bring brunch."

Joe smiled. "Thanks, Brandon."

"Hey, you sat with me in a hospital after a psychopath tried to turn me into Swiss cheese. This is the least I can do."

Joe laughed, saying his goodbyes and ending the call.

"Hey, Laura," he called out to the hallway as

he put on his shoes. "Brandon and Andrea are coming over and bringing food. So it's okay for you to leave your rightful place in the kitchen for a little bit."

He waited for a smart-aleck remark from her but got no response.

Joe chuckled. Obviously she hadn't heard him because there was no way Laura would let that slide.

He bounded down the stairs. "You're not waiting to clock me with a frying pan, right?"

Still nothing. He would be worried that Laura was truly irritated but knew it would take more than one silly sentence to get her mad. It was one of the things Joe liked most about her: her sense of humor.

But that didn't mean she wasn't about to jump out and pour a bucket of water over his head or something.

"Okay, I surrender." He held his arms up in front of him as he entered the kitchen. "I promise I will do all the cooking for the rest of our lives if you don't kill me now."

Actually he would do that for the rest of their lives if Laura would agree to share hers with him. Maybe he should start trying to get her to agree to those terms.

She wasn't in the kitchen.

Now things were a little weird.

"Hey, Laura?"

He poked his head around the corner to see if the bathroom door was closed, but it wasn't.

All humor fled. *Where was she?*

"Laura? Answer me, honey."

She wouldn't hide from him in jest, not now, not in the situation they were in. Joe pulled the door open to the garage, but she wasn't there. He systematically searched each room. Laura wasn't anywhere on the ground floor.

He ran back up the stairs to make sure she wasn't in one of the rooms up there. Nothing.

He entered the bedroom where they'd spent the entire night together.

His eyes flew to the nightstand.

His Glock was missing.

It had been there when he'd gone into the shower; he knew that for a fact. He'd grabbed his phone and brought it into the bathroom with him, not wanting to take a chance on missing a call from Steve if they found Bailey Heath.

Had Laura taken his gun for some reason? Why would she do that?

Joe slipped the phone from his pocket. He hit redial. Brandon answered just seconds later.

"Brandon, Laura's missing."

"What? Are you sure?"

"She's not anywhere in the house. It had to have happened in the last twenty minutes. While I was in the shower, or when I called you."

He heard Brandon murmur something.

"Joe, don't touch anything. I'll call Steve and

let him know what's going on. Andrea and I will be at Laura's house in five minutes."

Joe didn't say anything, just disconnected the call. He ran back down the stairs to look at the kitchen again.

His heart plummeted when he saw the cups of coffee that had been knocked over on the table. The only signs of struggle whatsoever.

But they were definitely signs of struggle.

Laura had been taken.

A maniac who had sworn revenge on Joe now had the one person he cared about most.

Joe tried to remain calm, but rage and terror fought for dominance inside him. All he could see were visions of dead women left for him to find. Stabbed, lying in pools of their own blood.

That could not happen to Laura. Joe couldn't survive if it did.

Chapter Nineteen

After last night with Joe, Laura had decided she just wasn't going to worry so much about their relationship anymore.

She had to face the facts: she was in love with him. Had been in love with him six years ago. Was still in love with him now. Worrying about their relationship wasn't going to change that.

In the six years she and Joe were apart, Laura had dated. Had even gotten a little serious with a couple of guys. But it had never worked out.

Because they weren't Joe.

And it didn't have a single thing to do with his money. Joe could work at the local 7-Eleven and

Laura would still love him. She wanted him despite his money, not because of it.

So she wasn't going to worry about it anymore. If Joe changed his mind in two months again, decided a serious relationship wasn't for him—*again*—Laura would have to deal with it.

She rubbed a hand across her chest. It would hurt—God, how it would hurt—but she would deal with it.

Right now she just wanted to concentrate on keeping him out of jail. Joe would call Brandon when he got out of the shower and get his opinion about turning himself in to the police. Brandon was a brilliant attorney; she and Joe both would be fools not to listen to his advice.

But first coffee. After the night she and Joe had shared—she smiled just a little thinking about it: her boyfriend was so dreamy—they needed the coffee. Laura made her way down the stairs.

She got the coffeepot going and stood next

to it with two mugs in hand. She heard some thumping upstairs over the sound of the water and rolled her eyes. What was Joe doing, break dancing in the shower? She wouldn't put it past him.

A minute later she could breathe in the blessed caffeinated aroma and soon poured two cups, turning to set them on the small kitchen table.

Right behind it stood Bailey Heath. A gun in her hand pointed straight at Laura.

Laura jerked and knocked one cup over, vaguely feeling the burning liquid slopping onto her hand. The rest of it spilled onto the table.

"What are you doing here?"

The woman looked dirty, unkempt. Madness danced in her eyes.

"I'm here for you. I'm here to make Joe pay. He has to burn like Tyler did. Joe took Tyler away from me."

Tyler. Summer Worrall's husband. The man who had gotten a restraining order against Bailey. Joe hadn't taken Tyler away from Bailey. He'd never been hers to begin with.

Of course pointing out any of that probably wasn't a good idea.

But Laura knew she needed to stall.

"Joe's upstairs in the shower. Why don't we wait for him to come down and we can talk about it."

Bailey shook her head. "No, the time for talking is over. It's now time to burn. You need to come with me."

"What if I don't?"

"Then I'll kill you right here. Since this is Joe's own gun, I'm sure that will be enough to put him in jail for a long time, right?" Bailey brought the gun up so it was pointed right at Laura's head. "Your choice."

Laura nodded. She couldn't see any way around it. It was better to give Joe time to find her than for him to come down now and discover her dead.

Laura knocked over the other coffee cup, trying to get any signal she could to Joe that there was a problem. Bailey's eyes narrowed as she cracked Laura in the back of the head with the gun. It wasn't hard enough to make her lose consciousness, but Laura still cried out at the throbbing in her skull.

Bailey grabbed her arm. "Let's go. And if you try anything on the way out, I will kill you. Killing you in the street then watching Joe find you will be much more satisfying than watching him find those other women. He didn't care about them at all."

Pain rocketed through Laura's arm from Bailey's punishing grip as she pulled her down the hallway and out the front door. Laura tried to figure out how the woman had even gotten into her house at all. The front door they'd just gone through had been locked. She and Joe had checked all the doors.

Bailey pulled her across the street and into the

very van Joe had found so suspicious the day before. He'd been right; it didn't belong there.

Bailey threw Laura in and stepped in behind her. Laura winced as Bailey bound her arms behind her back.

"Time to go."

Bailey was crazy. Being this close, Laura could smell the woman's body odor. She obviously hadn't showered in at least a couple of days. Laura couldn't help but make a face.

"Do I smell?" Bailey asked. "Hiding in vans and attics will do that. Showers aren't easy to come by."

"You've been in my attic?" So she hadn't gotten through locked doors.

"Ever since all Joe's little friends left yesterday. It's not comfortable, but it works."

Laura just stared at the other woman. She obviously couldn't be reasoned with.

"The Goldman brothers were supposed to snatch you and lure Joe out. I would've been able to kill you both then and blame it on them, but they couldn't even get you out of the parking garage." She rolled her eyes in disgust.

Bailey pulled a piece of cloth from a shelf and wrapped it around Laura's mouth as a gag.

"I lost you for a couple of days, but then picked you back up again when you showed up at the Goldmans' apartment. I've been watching you both ever since, waiting for a time to plant myself in your house."

Bailey shoved Laura to the side. Without her hands free to catch herself she fell hard onto the van's floor.

"It's time for Joe to pay for what he did to Tyler. I've been waiting a very long time for this. Your death right in front of him will just be the icing on the cake."

Bailey smiled. A bright, beautiful one, like she'd received a precious gift.

If Laura had any doubts that smile erased them all: Bailey Heath was a psychopath.

"We've got one more stop to make before I call Joe and the game begins." Bailey pulled out a canvas sack and placed it over Laura's head, cutting off her vision. "Although I'm not sure it can be called a game. Not when there's no chance of anyone winning except me."

Laura struggled to breathe through the gag. Through the panic. The other women Bailey had killed had just been a warm-up. Killing Laura while Joe watched would be the grand finale.

And Laura had no idea how Joe could possibly stop her.

JOE WOULD NEVER doubt he was part of the Omega team again.

They showed up in minutes.

They *all* showed up to help figure out what had happened to Laura.

Steve had arrived not long after Brandon and Andrea. Joe knew investigating a crime scene wasn't his strength, so he just tried to stay out of the way.

Joe couldn't stop staring at the spilled cups of coffee. They were the only signs of struggle at all. If it wasn't for them, he might have thought Laura had just decided to get out. Get as far from the situation—and him—as she could.

He wished like hell that was the case as he attempted to keep his panic pushed down.

Joe had already called his non–law enforcement contact Deacon Crandall. Explained as briefly as possible what had happened. He promised Crandall a million dollars if he had any part whatsoever in finding Laura alive. Another million to the individual who gave Deacon the tip.

Joe would keep offering a million dollars until he ran out of money or they found Laura. Because every dollar he had meant nothing without her.

Steve and Brandon stepped over to Joe.

"We think Bailey Heath was hiding in the attic.

We're not sure for how long." Brandon rested a hand on Joe's shoulder. "There's no sign of a forced entry at all. And Laura definitely would not have just opened the door to Bailey."

"We found some pieces of insulation from the attic on the floor, suggesting that the pull-down door had been opened recently," Steve continued. "And a hole had been drilled through the door. Probably so Bailey could see and hear at least part of what was going on in the house."

Joe thought his rage had capped out, but he'd been wrong. The thought of a sicko like Bailey Heath listening and watching him and Laura last night sickened him. His hands tightened into fists.

"As best we can tell she just waited." Brandon squeezed his shoulder. "Once you were in the shower and Laura was alone, Bailey made her way out and took her."

Joe's curse was low and pointed.

Steve nodded. "She probably had another

weapon. Taking your gun was just a more convenient method of framing you."

For when Bailey decided to kill Laura. Steve didn't say it but they were all thinking it.

Joe could feel the panic working its way up his chest.

"Joe." Brandon stood in front of Joe, placing both hands on his shoulders. "I have every confidence that Laura is still alive. If Bailey Heath had just wanted to frame you, she would've shot Laura and left her here in the house. It would've fit the MO of the other crimes and would've almost certainly landed you in jail."

Joe could hear Brandon's logic, knew he was probably right, but still couldn't get the terror under control.

"Bailey has some sort of elaborate plan," Brandon continued. "It's the only logical reason for her taking Laura out of the house."

"We will figure out how to beat Bailey at her

own game. I promise you that," Steve said, sincerity clear in the man's eyes.

Joe nodded, and Brandon dropped his hold. "I just want Laura back. I have money. I know you guys know that, but I'm talking about cash I can have available in minutes if that will help. I'm willing to use other channels if it means getting Laura back safely."

Criminal channels. Mercenary channels. Joe didn't care what side of the law they were on.

"Joe, don't. Don't turn to illegal pathways." Steve took something out of his pocket. Joe looked down and realized it was Joe's Omega badge and official weapon.

Steve handed him the items. "You're part of this team. Part of this family. Give us every opportunity to get her back before making decisions you might regret."

Joe nodded. He wouldn't rein in Deacon Crandall, mostly because he trusted the man to stay on the right side of the law if he possibly could. Joe wouldn't move into dark territory.

Yet.

More of the Omega team showed up at Laura's front door. "I'm going to handle everybody here," Steve said. "Send them to HQ. A crime lab team is coming to process the house. Everyone else needs to get to work, pressing in harder to find Bailey Heath and Laura."

Steve walked over to the rest of his team.

"You going to be able to keep it together?" Brandon asked Joe.

"As long as I know she's alive, I'll keep it together. Hell, as long as I think there is any possible chance Laura is alive, I'll keep it together." He had to. For her.

Brandon nodded.

Joe looked down at the badge in his hand. "But I can't promise not to work outside the law on this, Brandon. Not if it means getting her back safely. I don't care if I lose everything—money, job, even my freedom."

Joe saw Brandon looking at Andrea across the room.

"What would you do if a psycho had Andrea?"

A psycho had held Andrea in his grip just a month ago. Brandon had nearly died trying to save her.

"Absolutely anything," Brandon said softly. "Pay any price. Employ any measure. Become someone I don't even recognize."

Joe knew he would do exactly the same.

Chapter Twenty

Back at Omega Headquarters the Critical Response Division team worked like the well-oiled machine they were. Joe remembered the van, which was now gone, and Derek Waterman found it on a traffic camera in the area of Laura's house at a time fitting when Laura had been taken.

Joe computed the distance of that traffic light from Laura's house and the time the van sped through the light.

He rammed his fist down on the desk next to Derek.

"Damn it."

"What?" Derek took his eyes off the screen to look over at Joe.

Joe rubbed his hand over his face. "In order for them to be at that light at that time, I must have just missed them. If I had just run outside instead of checking the rest of the house…"

Derek shrugged. "Checking the house first was the right call. I would've done the same."

But the thought that he could've stopped it burned like acid in Joe's gut.

Derek and Ashton Fitzgerald, another member of Omega's specialized tactical team, continued the search for the van, splitting the work and using different cameras in different directions. They followed as long as they could but eventually lost it when cameras became more scarce as the van headed out of town.

Which meant Laura and Bailey could be anywhere west of Colorado Springs. Unless, of course, Bailey had thought they might catch her on camera and circled back.

A dead end.

Jon, Brandon and Andrea continued their pro-file of Bailey Heath, digging further into people Bailey had known. It would be helpful, but so far was just another dead end.

Others on the team watched the footage again from his crime scenes trying to pick out any-thing they might have missed watching it the last two days.

Joe was about to go out of his mind without something concrete to put his energy toward. When the crime lab team called into headquar-ters with some questions, Joe felt almost relieved to have to go back to Laura's house to clarify some things.

"Lillian is going to go with you," Steve told him. "We're not leaving you unprotected in case Bailey decides to make you a target also."

Joe nodded down at Lillian. The tiny woman could kick someone's ass more ways than most people could learn in a lifetime. She might not look like protection detail, but Joe trusted her.

"Okay. Let's go." He prayed the crime scene crew would have something that gave them a clue to where Laura was. Every minute Bailey had her was a minute too long.

When they got to Laura's house, Joe could see the lab workers were doing a thorough job. Every inch of the attic, where Bailey had been hiding, had been searched. They ran what they could through a portable computer system at the scene. The rest would be done back at Omega headquarters.

Getting a hair sample from Joe helped them eliminate his DNA from all possible evidence sources. A pregnant Molly Humpfries-Waterman, Derek's wife, oversaw it all.

Joe answered all her questions about when Bailey could've gotten into the house and the van he'd seen outside. The crew sent someone to gather evidence in that area also.

"We're going to find something, Joe." Molly stroked his arm. "We'll get some sort of reading from all this. Some direction to send you."

But would it be in time?

Because this was also starting to look like another dead end. Like it couldn't get much worse.

Then the doorbell rang followed by a pounding on the door.

"Colorado Springs Police Department. We need you to open the door. We have a warrant for the arrest of Joe Matarazzo."

Joe let out a bitter string of obscenities and met Molly's eyes. "They still think I'm responsible for the deaths of the other women."

"And Laura being missing isn't going to help your case."

He nodded. "I can't let them take me right now. They'll confiscate my phone. What if Bailey calls? Or Laura? I'm going out the back."

Lillian moved silently from the rear of the room to Joe and Molly. "No, you're not. They've got uniformed cops coming up the back. No way out that way."

"Damn it." Joe slammed his fist against the wall.

"Steve will make some calls. He'll have you out as soon as possible. Hopefully in just a few hours." But Molly's eyes were worried. So were Lillian's.

The cops banged on the door again. All the Omega techs stared at Joe, unsure what to do.

"Bailey didn't kill Laura here. If she wanted just to frame me she could've killed Laura here with my own gun and it would've been the perfect setup."

Molly nodded. "I hate to admit it, but I agree."

"Everything in my gut tells me Bailey is going to contact me. Make some trade of me for Laura." Or something worse.

"You and I can try to strong-arm our way out," Lillian said. "We're outmanned and outgunned by the locals, but we might make it."

Joe considered it for just a moment. He squeezed Lillian's shoulder. "Thanks for the offer, killer. If I thought it would work, I might try."

He reached in and got his phone out of his pocket and handed it to Lillian. "Keep this. Better Omega has it than the cops, for when Bailey contacts me. Because she will."

Lillian took it. More banging on the door. A threat to enter the premises using force.

"There's a contact in there, Deacon Crandall," Joe told Lillian. "He's aware of the situation and is willing to color outside the lines if and when needed. Tell him it's probably needed. Especially if Steve can't get me out fast enough."

Lillian nodded. "We're not going to let you sit in some cell while this is going down, Joe. Believe that."

He sure as hell hoped he could. He walked quickly over to answer the door before the police decided to ram it down. He opened it, immediately met by Detective Thompson, the same man who had questioned him before.

"I'm here, Detective. No need to shoot the door down or anything."

Thompson looked a little sheepish. Perhaps they'd been about to do just that.

"Why didn't you answer?" He looked around at the crime scene investigators still working. "What's going on here?"

Joe sure as hell wasn't going to mention Laura's kidnapping if he didn't have to. He was sure Thompson would immediately add that to the list of crimes to charge Joe with.

"We're looking for possible evidence to help us find the woman who is trying to frame me for the murders of my ex-girlfriends. The real villain in this situation's name is Bailey Heath, if you happen to care."

Thompson raised an eyebrow. "You'd be surprised at how many people claim they're being framed when the police come to arrest them."

Molly joined Joe at his side. "I'm Dr. Molly Humphries-Waterman. I am the head of the crime lab at Omega Sector. I assure you that what Joe says is true. He is not the one who killed those women."

"I'm sorry, but I have a warrant for his arrest. If there is proof he didn't commit the murders, I'm sure he'll be out in no time." Thompson looked around. "Where's your lawyer?"

"She's not here at the moment."

"After the way she busted my chops at the station for questioning you, I would assume she would want to read this over before I take you in."

Joe was thankful for everyone's silence. "Doubtless. But she had business that couldn't be delayed so she's not here. I'll read the warrant myself."

Joe took the paper, well aware he was stalling. Molly had turned to the side and immediately called Steve to see what could be done. He didn't see Lillian anywhere.

"I'll need your weapon, your badge and your cell phone."

Molly looked over from her phone call. "He needs a warrant in order to go through your phone."

"Phone is listed on the warrant." Thompson grinned, beady eyes narrowed. He obviously took a great deal of pleasure lording his power over Joe.

Joe handed his weapon and badge. "I don't have a cell phone with me."

"Quit screwing around, Matarazzo. I know you have a phone."

Joe shrugged. "You're welcome to search me. Search the entire place. I lost my cell phone."

Thompson shoved Joe toward the wall. "I was trying to be nice, but if that's the way you want to play it… Hands against the wall."

Thompson searched Joe, obviously not believing him about the phone. When he didn't find anything he pulled out a pair of handcuffs.

"Is that absolutely necessary?" Molly asked. "We're all on the same side here, Detective Thompson. It won't be long until Omega gets the evidence over to your precinct exonerating Joe."

"No offense, ma'am, but until that happens, this guy—" he jerked Joe forward "—and I are not on the same side. I work for a living. Very hard. I don't think a jerk like this truly understands that concept at all. He thinks he can do whatever he wants."

Concern flew across Molly's features, "Detective—"

"It's okay, Molly," Joe cut in. "You stay here and work. Get the info we need. And tell Steve to hurry up and get me the hell out of Colorado Springs' finest's custody."

Molly nodded and Thompson led Joe out to the squad car, putting him in the backseat. Joe didn't say what was on his mind because Thompson didn't know about Laura's kidnapping, but his thoughts were dark.

If Laura died because of the detective's refusal to see beyond his own prejudice when it came to Joe, Joe would spend the rest of his life making sure Thompson had good reason to feel prejudice against him. He wouldn't physically hurt the man, but he could make his life a living hell in many other ways.

Joe sat in the squad car a long time before they began the drive from Fountain north toward Colorado Springs. The farther away they drove Joe from the action, the larger the ball of acid grew in his gut.

Lillian had his phone. She would get it back to Steve, or whoever, at Omega. If Bailey called—*when* Bailey called—someone would be able to talk to her. What exactly they would say to an obvious psychopath, Joe had no idea. He just hoped they could reason with her, explain the situation.

He hoped Bailey would believe them and not hurt Laura because of something completely out of her control.

"How's it feel sitting back there?" Thompson gave a deep, satisfied sigh. "All your money isn't going to help you now. You're going to jail, Matarazzo. And I'm going to be known as the one who put you there."

"The only thing you're going to be known as is the jerk who couldn't see reason when it sat six inches from his face."

Thompson rolled his eyes. "Be sure to tell that to your cell mate. I'm sure he'll think it's a lovely story."

Joe ignored Thompson. Fighting with him wouldn't accomplish anything. Hopefully Lillian had gotten in touch with Deacon and the man would have the best lawyer in the state—

second to Laura, of course—waiting for them when Joe arrived.

Or he would have some blackmail info on someone who could get him released. Joe had learned long ago that Deacon worked on the side of justice, not necessarily the law. Deacon knew Laura's life was in danger, knew Joe wasn't guilty, knew his arrest might cause her further harm.

If Steve couldn't get Joe released through proper channels, Deacon would make sure it happened other ways.

Joe just hoped it would be in time.

The detention building was in the northeast section of town. Joe watched as they got off I-25 onto the smaller back roads. Past the airport, in a relatively deserted section of town, they came to a red light. It turned green but an armored car, stopped in front of them, didn't move.

Even this small delay increased Joe's frustration. They needed to get to the station immediately so someone could get him out. Had Bailey called? Not knowing was killing him.

Another armored truck pulled up directly beside them and stopped, effectively blocking Thompson from being able to go around the vehicle in front of them.

"What the hell?" Thompson murmured.

The detective honked but neither vehicle moved.

"They have engine problems, Thompson. Just reverse and go around for God's sake."

Joe wasn't expecting a third vehicle to come up behind them and physically hit their car. The jolt rammed him into the seat in front of him.

Thompson cursed as two masked men ran up to the car, their guns pointed clearly at him and the uniformed officer riding next to him.

"Out of the car. Now!" one masked man—the one pointing his weapon at Thompson—said. The other kept his gun silently pointed at the other cop.

Thompson looked back at him. "Do you have something to do with this, Matarazzo?"

"What the hell are you talking about? How could I have something to do with this?" Was it people working for Bailey Heath? Had she been watching Laura's house then sent someone to finish the job?

"Get out of the car. Right now." The man shot at the engine. Everybody in the car jumped.

Thompson was sweating. "Okay, fine, fine."

Thompson and the uniformed officer opened the door and before either man could get completely out and to their feet, both the masked guys reached over and injected them quickly with something in their necks. Thompson and the cop fell unconscious onto the street.

The guy who'd spoken to Thompson reached down and got the detective's keys, then unlocked the back door. He pulled Joe out roughly and put a sack over his head.

"Let's go, Mr. Matarazzo." His voice was clear

and menacing. "I hope whoever is in charge of your bank account is willing to pay or you're a dead man. Of course, you're probably a dead man anyway."

Chapter Twenty-One

The man dragged Joe over to the armored car that had stopped behind them and threw him in the back. He hit hard, unable to catch himself. Damn Thompson for insisting on handcuffing Joe.

"Don't kill him for God's sake. That defeats the purpose."

A woman's voice. Bailey Heath's?

The door slammed in the back of the armored car and they began moving.

"You alright there, Joe? Your man Deacon is quite the prince." Joe was shocked to find Lillian at his side helping him sit up and taking the bag off his head.

He couldn't stop his gaping stare. "What in the world? I thought you guys were kidnapping me. Working for Bailey Heath. That was a pretty elaborate ruse." Lillian unlocked his handcuffs and Joe rubbed his wrists where they'd chafed against the metal.

"We had to make them believe it was an actual kidnapping, so you can't be charged with anything later." Deacon had removed his mask and was now driving the armored car away from the scene.

"I'm assuming Thompson and the cop will be okay?" Joe didn't think he'd lose much sleep over it either way.

"They'll be out another thirty minutes. I wasn't sure if there were any recording devices in the squad car, so I kept up the act just in case."

Lillian shook her head. "Yeah, not because you enjoy breaking the law and risking your life. That would be crazy."

Deacon looked back at them and winked. "Anything worth doing is worth overdoing."

Lillian rolled her eyes and glanced over at Joe. "That's some friend you have there. Questionable moral compass."

Joe just shrugged. He didn't care about Deacon's moral compass, at least not in this case. They'd gotten Joe out without anyone getting hurt.

"Thanks you guys. I don't know how you pulled it off this fast, but you're amazing."

"Wait until you get the bill. You might not think me so amazing then."

Joe couldn't care less about the money.

"Were there any calls on my phone while you had it?"

Lillian shook her head. "No. I'm sorry."

She removed the overalls she had on over her clothes. "We've got to ditch this truck before Colorado Springs' finest wake up. We need to get you deep inside Omega where they can't look for you."

"I've already got it set up. Car ready for you." A few minutes later Deacon pulled up to a parking garage. "This is where I leave you, kids." He tossed keys to Lillian.

"Deacon—" Joe couldn't find the words to express the size of his gratitude as he got out of the back of the armored car and walked around to the driver's side.

"Another time, boss. I've still got a lot of feelers out all over about your woman. Hopefully you'll hear from me again soon. Right now I need to finish cleaning up this mess."

He winked at Lillian, who just glared at him, and drove off.

Lillian drove the most direct route to Omega headquarters. It wouldn't be long before the police either reported Joe missing or reported him as a fugitive. He didn't care which. He was just glad to be back actively participating in finding Laura again.

In the end none of their work helped them find Bailey Heath. Bailey decided she wanted to be found. Joe and Lillian had been back an hour when he received the call on his phone. The bustle of search tactics fell silent. Joe's phone had already been connected to a recording device. He turned it on speaker so everyone could hear.

"Hello."

"It's time for us to talk face-to-face, don't you think?"

Joe had never heard Bailey Heath's voice, and found it shrill and annoying.

Or maybe that was just because he wanted to kill her so badly.

"Is Laura alive?"

Bailey laughed. "I'm glad I finally found someone you actually care about, Joe. I was afraid I'd have to kill all your ex-girlfriends before I got the reaction I wanted."

Steve nodded at Joe. They were recording this. Bailey had pretty much just admitted to the murders and cleared Joe's name. At least now he wouldn't have to worry about the Colorado Springs police coming after him again.

But he noticed Bailey hadn't answered the question. "Bailey, is Laura alive? This conversation doesn't go any further until I have that information."

"Yes, she's alive. For now."

"Let me talk to her."

There were a few moments of silence. Was Laura dead and Bailey was attempting to figure out what lie to tell?

"Now, Bailey. Let me talk to her now."

He had to know.

"Fine." Bailey's voice became shriller.

He could hear murmuring and something brushing against the phone, obviously from Bailey's movements.

"Joe?"

He almost dropped to his knees in relief from hearing Laura's voice.

"Laura, has she hurt you?"

"No, I'm fine but she has—"

Joe heard the thud of flesh against flesh before Laura cried out.

"Laura?" No one answered. "Laura!"

A few moments later Bailey came back on the phone. "No more talking to her. Laura is, um, unavailable."

Joe closed his eyes and took deep breaths to remain calm. Laura was alive. That was the most important thing.

Thinking of ways to kill Bailey Heath was secondary.

"What do you want, Bailey?"

"A simple trade. You for Laura."

"Fine. Deal." He didn't even hesitate. He would give himself to this madwoman a thousand times over if it meant Laura's safety. "But only if Laura is alive. Do you understand?"

She rattled off an address. "You have thirty minutes. And no press that you love so much, Joe. No cameras. Not like when you allowed Tyler to be killed. And none of your friends either. If I see anyone but you, Laura dies."

"Fine." Joe had no problem telling the lie.

"You remember how Tyler died, don't you, Joe?"

"Yes." He had the burn scars to remind him every day.

"It would be a shame for Laura to die the same way. To burn."

Joe grimaced. "I'll come alone, Bailey. Just don't hurt her."

"See you soon."

As soon as Joe hung up, Steve reached over and grabbed Joe by his shirt collar. "Don't you say one damn word about going in there alone, you got it?"

"You heard what Bailey said."

"That woman is planning to kill you, Joe. It

is obvious to every person in here. She aims to kill you and Laura, too."

Joe looked around the room. Everyone nodded.

"Trust us to do our job," Steve continued, his hands on Joe's shoulders now rather than his shirt. "You get in there with Bailey, buy us time to get in position. If she gives you Laura, great, we'll get her out immediately and then get you out. Maybe you can even talk Bailey into surrendering and nobody has to get hurt."

Joe closed his eyes. His boss was right. Bailey wasn't planning to let anyone live, least of all Joe and Laura. She wanted to hurt him in any way she could.

"I'll buy you the time with Bailey that you need." Joe opened his eyes. "But you promise to get Laura out first."

"Absolutely."

"Then let's go. We'll need almost the entire thirty minutes to get there."

"Alright, people." Steve walked as he spoke. "We're wheels up in five. Security alert red.

And somebody get a copy of that recording to whoever Jack Thompson's boss is at Colorado Springs PD. Plus, tell them that Joe fought off his 'kidnappers' and is with us."

Everybody moved at Steve's words. Activity buzzed instantly.

"We've already pulled up the building plans," Lillian said. "SWAT will study en route."

"We need the best plan we can formulate before we get there," Steve said. "Give Joe the smallest earpiece we have."

Joe shook his head. "But what if Bailey sees it?"

"She won't. But we have to be able to communicate with you. To let you know when we've got Laura out."

Joe nodded. There were so many things that could go wrong with this mission it was difficult to consider them all.

LAURA LAY ON the ground, blood pooling in her mouth. Bailey had taken off the gag and sack to let Laura talk to Joe.

They were in some sort of warehouse or old factory or something. A large, dirty building with rafters in the high ceiling and dust on the ground.

She had wanted to get Joe information—what little of it she had—but all that had gotten Laura was a bruised face and a hard fall to the ground.

She'd tried to warn Joe he was about to walk into a trap. That there was someone else involved.

Bailey had stopped somewhere and picked up another person. Laura didn't know who—the person hadn't talked at all, and Bailey had turned the radio up so loud in the van that no one could hear anything.

Laura looked around. The person wasn't here now. Was he or she waiting to ambush Joe? Was it someone who would be keeping an eye out for the rest of the Omega team and notifying Bailey if anyone else came with Joe?

Laura hoped beyond all hope that Joe would

accept help from his teammates. Otherwise he had no chance to survive this.

Laura watched Bailey douse some discarded piles of wood on the ground with gasoline.

She wasn't sure Joe had a chance even with the rest of the team.

"Don't worry. Everything else is already soaked with one sort of accelerant or another. I've had a year to study fire and know exactly what works best." A blissful smile lit Bailey's face. "Once fire touches anywhere in this building, it will only take minutes for flames to engulf it entirely."

Bailey planned to die today. And she planned to take Laura and Joe with her.

Laura tried to scoot back when Bailey walked over to her with her can of gas, but with her hands still bound behind her back, there was nowhere to go.

"No, don't—"

She stopped talking so she wouldn't get gas in her mouth as Bailey poured it on her.

"Trust me. It's better this way. It will be much quicker." Laura flinched as Bailey smoothed a piece of gas-soaked hair away from Laura's face. "But now it's time to get you in place. I'm sure Joe and his friends will be here early if they can manage it."

"But you told Joe to come alone."

Bailey rolled her eyes. "I've been watching that group for a year. They're not going to let Joe go into this building alone. He'll try to stall me while they look for you. It's like SWAT 101."

Laura realized that's exactly what would happen. "So you're going to take on all of Omega Sector?"

"No, although I have to admit, I wish I could've figured out what member of the SWAT team was responsible for not taking the shot at the man who killed Tyler. They must have had a sharpshooter somewhere who didn't do what he needed to do. I would like for that person to burn also." She shrugged. "But you take what you can get."

"What's to keep them from just shooting you, storming in and rescuing me?"

Bailey smiled. "They'll consider it. But they won't know where you are. They'll think they know where you are, but they won't."

Laura had no idea what Bailey was talking about. She was beginning to wonder if Bailey even knew what she was talking about.

"You'll be right here." Bailey walked a few steps past Laura and opened a hatch in the floor.

Laura tried to scoot away again as Bailey reached for her. She couldn't hold in the groan of pain from her sore arms and shoulders as Bailey dragged her across the floor. Bailey stopped just as they got to the hatch. She took the gag back out of her pocket and tied it back in Laura's mouth.

"You'll be right here where all the action is, but they'll never know it."

Laura screamed as Bailey pushed her into the hatch, tears coming to her eyes as she hit the ground hard even though it was only two feet down.

"See? It's not deep. Some sort of false floor." Bailey jumped in with Laura and tied her feet together. Then grabbed a strange-looking poncho. "This material blocks your heat signature. So when Joe's friends are trying to find you, you won't show up on their equipment."

Bailey tucked Laura's legs under it. "Plus, I've given them something else to chase. They'll be happy about that. I'm not a complete monster, you know."

Laura longed to ask Bailey what the hell she was talking about.

"Bad thing about this material is that it may smother you if you're left under it too long." Bailey shrugged apologetically as she tucked it around Laura like a cocoon. "But honestly, I think the fire will get you before that."

Bailey pulled the material up and over Laura's head.

"Don't worry. It will all be over soon."

Laura didn't even try to answer. She just focused on breathing in and out in the darkness. She heard the hatch door close, but that didn't change her focus.

She had to stay calm. Had to keep breathing. Had to stay alive until Joe got here.

And pray he could outsmart a maniac.

Chapter Twenty-Two

Joe drove Steve's SUV, which allowed Derek and Steve to sit low in the backseats and not be noticeable. Under any other circumstances Joe would've found it pretty funny to see his boss and friend twisted like pretzels to fit their large frames near the floor of the vehicle.

Joe couldn't find anything humorous right now.

Two other Omega vehicles approached the address Bailey gave Joe—an abandoned lumber house that had last been used over fifty years ago—from a different direction. Steve had on the speakerphone so they all could coordinate.

"The building has some pretty vast square footage," Ashton Fitzgerald, a SWAT team member, announced. "Terrible for us, tactically."

"So heat signatures are our best bet?" Steve asked.

"Definitely," Derek responded. "Joe, you've got to keep Bailey talking. Give us a chance to find Laura and get her out."

"I will."

Joe tuned out as the SWAT team spoke back and forth to each other. Who would be coming in from what direction. That wasn't Joe's job. He'd trust that the team would have his back when he needed them.

Joe's job was damn near impossible. To go in, look Bailey Heath in the eye and pretend like he gave a damn about anything she had to say.

The only thing he cared about was finding Laura.

He could still hear her cry of pain as Bailey

had obviously struck her. His fists gripped the steering wheel tighter.

"You okay, Joe?" Steve asked from the back.

"What if she's dead? That would've been a smart play on Bailey's part, right? Letting me talk to Laura and then killing her?"

"Don't go down that road. It leads nowhere," Steve told him. "We go into every hostage situation as if we can get everyone out alive. This is no different."

But it was different. It was Laura.

"You have to go in there with a cool head. Keep your training in place. Talk to Bailey like you would any other hostage-taker. I know it's hard but it's what you have to do."

Joe took a deep breath. "Okay."

"I've seen you walk into situations I would've sworn no one was coming out of alive. But you've gotten everyone out. You've listened to people as if you were their psychiatrist or priest or something. You've given them a chance to be heard. Give that to Bailey Heath."

"Hell, Steve. She's hurt Laura. I don't know if I can."

Derek knew what it was to have a psychopath hurt his woman and not be able to do anything about it. "Then you listen to Bailey not because you give a damn about her, but because it will give us time to get Laura out. We'll get her out, Joe."

Joe prayed that was true. "Alright. We're almost there."

"Pull to the side," Steve said. "I'll direct from here. Derek will join the rest of the SWAT team once we've figured out where Laura is."

"It will take us a while to manually scan a building this big, Joe. Buy us as much time as you can."

Joe took his weapon and waist holster off and put it in the passenger seat beside him. "See you guys on the flip side." He opened his door.

"We'll get her, Joe."

Steve's voice was the last thing he heard before closing the door. Joe didn't care about his own safety. Only getting Laura back. He was glad Steve and the team understood that.

He found the door and allowed his eyes to adjust to the dimness of the building before walking any farther inside.

"Bailey, I'm here," he called out. "Where are you?"

The place seemed even more vast from the inside. Bailey could be lying in wait any number of places. She could step out at any minute, dump Laura's dead body at his feet and shoot him between the eyes.

The only thing stopping her was her need for the theatrical. For Joe to burn. It wasn't a comforting thought.

He could smell the accelerants all around him. He had no doubt Bailey planned for this place to go up in flames.

"C'mon, Bailey. We can't talk if I don't know where you are."

He heard a disturbing cackle from deeper inside the lumber house. Joe began walking toward it.

"I don't know that I really want to talk," Bailey said. He couldn't see her, but could tell he was heading in the right direction.

"But you wanted me here."

"But not necessarily to talk. More to watch you burn. And your girlfriend, too."

Joe sucked in a breath and forced himself to remain calm. "Is Laura alive?"

The question was more to keep Bailey talking than to gather information. He knew he couldn't trust anything she said.

"I think so."

"What does that mean?" Joe kept walking toward Bailey's high-pitched voice.

"She's alive. I want to hurt you, not her."

"Unfortunately, I don't think that's true. You killed three other women I used to care about."

Bailey's voice was much closer now. She laughed. "Okay, you got me. I don't mind hurting her if it also hurts you. And you care much more about her than you did those other three. I was able to tell that easily."

Joe advanced into a room that looked like it was once an office. Bailey stepped out from behind the broken paneling of a wall. She had a gun in her hand. Probably still Joe's Glock.

"Hi, Joe." She smiled at him, but hatred burned in her eyes.

Along with a whole hell of a lot of crazy.

"Bailey. Where's Laura?"

"She's not here with me."

"I can see that." He fought to tamp down panic.

The tiny earpiece inside his left ear clicked on. Steve. *"That's an affirmative, Joe. There's only two heat signatures in the room you're in. You and Bailey. We're systematically searching the rest of the building."*

"Is Laura alive, Bailey?"

Bailey grimaced. "Yes. She's alive. For now."

"Let her go and you can do whatever you want to me."

Joe realized he meant it. He would die whatever agonizing death Bailey planned if it meant Laura would live.

"Oh, I have plans for you, Joe." Bailey smiled again. "Don't I get a striptease like the people did last week?"

"Are you worried I have weapons?"

"Not really. If you kill me you'll never find out where Laura is. And she will die. Of course, she's probably going to die anyway."

Joe had his first glimpse of hope that Laura was still alive. Bailey wanted drama. Maybe she planned to kill Laura in front of him as some big, painful gesture.

Let her have her plans. He would give the

team the time they needed to find Laura and thwart them.

"Sure, I'll take off my clothes, if that's what you really want. But I thought you loved Tyler. I wouldn't have thought you would want to see another man naked."

The earpiece switched on again. *"We've detected a faint heat signature. In the southwest corner of the building—it's the only one. It's a weird signal, but it's definitely a person. We're going to get her."*

"I don't want you to get completely naked, Joe. Just take off your shirt," Bailey sneered. "I want to see the burn marks from when Tyler died."

Joe began pulling his T-shirt over his head as the earpiece clicked on again. *"Ashton and Derek are trying to work their way to her. Keep Bailey talking."*

"Is this what you want?" Joe asked, walking over to her and turning his back so she could clearly see the burn scars that stretched down his neck and back. He flinched as she touched him.

"Did it hurt?"

Joe didn't know if he should lie or not. Wasn't sure what he should say to keep Bailey in the moment and give the team the time they needed.

He turned back to look at her and there was such a sadness in Bailey's eyes, he almost felt pity for her.

Bailey was crazy. Had ruined lives. Had killed people.

But she loved Tyler, and had lost him.

Joe tried to think of what he would say to Bailey if she wasn't holding the woman he loved captive.

What he would say to do his job.

"Yes, the burns hurt. But I'm sure my physical pain wasn't nearly as bad as what you went through by losing Tyler."

"Now you're just trying to manipulate me." She pointed the gun at him.

"I'll admit that was my plan coming in here. But now I'm not. Now I'm just trying to talk to you."

Bailey began to cry. "Why, Joe? Why couldn't you get Tyler out that day? I've watched you for a year now. I've seen you go into one situation after another and almost always get everyone out safely. Why couldn't you do that for Tyler?"

"I've asked myself that same question every day. If I could go back and change the past I would. Bring Tyler back for you."

Of course, Tyler would be going back to the wife he loved and his baby daughter, not to Bailey. But Joe didn't mention that.

His earpiece clicked again. *"Derek and Ashton are on the other side of a door where Laura is. But they are going to have to make some noise to get through it, and it will definitely alert Bailey that the rest of us are here."*

Once Bailey heard the noise she would certainly shoot Joe or herself or light the place on fire.

Could he talk Bailey down? Was she determined to kill him no matter what? He had to try.

"Let's hold on for a second."

"Roger that," Steve whispered.

"What?" Bailey asked, eyes narrowing.

"Let's hold on to the memories," Joe covered. "And I'm saying this not just for my sake, but for yours, too. Would Tyler want you to do this? To kill people?"

Bailey began pacing back and forth.

"I don't think Tyler would want you to pay that price, Bailey. To carry that weight."

She stopped pacing and looked at Joe. For the first time there was some semblance of clarity in her eyes.

"It's too late. I've already killed."

"It's not too late if you stop now. We can't do anything about the past. It's only the future we can change."

Bailey lowered her weapon and for just a moment Joe thought she might surrender. Looking at her he realized just how young she really was. Lost. Frightened. She hunched her shoulders and put her hands in her jacket pockets.

And something changed. Joe didn't know what or why, but when Bailey looked back up at him it was with complete resolve and determination.

All the crazy was back.

"No. It's too late. I'll do whatever it takes to avenge Tyler the way he would want me to."

She was going to kill Joe and herself and take Laura with them.

"Go, Steve, go," Joe said. No longer caring if the secret was out. Three seconds later a huge noise blasted through the air as the SWAT team took out the door at the other end of the building to rescue Laura.

He looked at Bailey expecting to see surprise or fear. She just smiled. Joe realized this had been her plan all along and somehow they had all just played into it perfectly.

"Sounds like your friends found her. Good.

Believe it or not, my fight was never with her. With them." Bailey took a deep breath, holding her arms out slightly as if she was breathing in a beautiful dawn.

Joe smelled it, too. The building was on fire.

Bailey looked at him, tilting her head sideways. "And now we burn."

Chapter Twenty-Three

Joe realized Bailey must have doused just about everything in accelerants. The place was going up fast.

He pressed a hand to his ear. "Steve, report. Do you have Laura?"

"Yes, Ashton has her. She's hurt, but alive. They're carrying her out. Busting the door must have triggered some sort of ignition. The whole building is burning."

Ashton tried to cut in on the frequency to tell Joe something, but there was too much noise from the fire. Joe couldn't understand him.

Laura was safe. That was all that mattered.

"Laura's out, Bailey. Your plan failed. You and I need to get out too before this whole building comes down around us."

She brought the gun back up and pointed it at him. "Actually you and I and the woman you love burning was the plan all along."

"Laura's already gone, Bailey. You'll have to try your plan another day."

After she'd spent three consecutive life sentences in prison.

"You might want to check with your boss there, Joe. Make sure everything is how you think it is."

Something about Bailey's calm expression sent a chill through him. He pressed the earpiece closer to his ear.

"Steve? I need you to confirm that you have Laura."

"Hold. Derek and Ashton are coming out of the building right now."

Joe heard lots of coughing then the distinct

sound of a baby crying. He pieced it together before he heard what Ashton had to tell Steve.

"This is Summer Worrall and her baby."

"Joe, we don't have Laura. I repeat, we don't have Laura."

Joe took the earpiece out of his ear and put it in his pocket. His friends couldn't help him now.

"You took Summer and the baby."

Bailey shrugged. "I didn't hurt her. Like I said, my fight was never with her. I understood why Tyler found it difficult to leave her. They'd taken vows."

"Where's Laura?" The smoke was getting thicker even though the fire wasn't near them yet.

Bailey stomped her foot and Joe looked down realizing there was a hatch door of sorts underneath her. "She's been with us all along. Wrapped in some material that made her heat signature invisible to your friends."

Joe took a step toward Bailey. She pointed

the gun at his head. "You can get her out, but slowly."

Joe nodded, praying Laura was still alive in there. He opened the hatch door and saw a form wrapped in a blanket unmoving. He jumped in and gently started unwrapping Laura.

She was covered in sweat, skin red and blotchy, her breathing shallow. The stench of gasoline permeated the air.

Bailey looked down from where she stood, gun still pointed at them. "Yeah, sorry. The price for hiding a heat signature is material that has been known to smother people."

Joe unwrapped the gag from Laura's mouth, wiping sweat from her brow. "Laura, are you okay? Sweetheart?"

Her eyes blinked open but didn't focus. "Joe."

"C'mon, let's get you out of here." He reached back and untied her arms, forcing his thumbs into the joints at the front of her shoulders to relax them enough that they could move after being held at such an awkward angle for so long. He knew it had to hurt—saw tears roll down her face—but she didn't make a sound. He untied her feet and climbed out of the hole with Laura in his arms.

Bailey had the gun pointed right at them. "See? I knew you loved her. I'm sorry I killed those other women because that was just a waste. Laura was the only one I needed to kill to make you feel my pain in losing Tyler."

Joe felt desperation swamp him. He could smell the smoke getting thicker. They didn't have much time.

He had to get Laura out of here. He turned his back to Bailey so he could talk to Laura in his arms.

"Laura." He shook her slightly, trying to get her to remain conscious. "Can you stand, baby? Walk? Open your eyes for me."

She did, her beautiful hazel eyes focused on him this time. "I need you to be able to walk, okay?" He set her on her feet when she nodded again.

He was going to make a deal with the devil and pray it was enough. He turned back to Bailey, one arm behind him to help Laura find strength to stand. This would only work if she could get herself out of here.

"You want me to burn, Bailey. I know you do." Joe knew exactly what Bailey needed to hear and was willing to give it to her. "I deserve to burn."

Bailey's eyes lit. "Yes, you do."

"I will stay here and burn with you. But you have to let Laura go. She's innocent."

"No!" Bailey pointed her gun at Laura.

Joe pulled Laura more fully behind him. She was still wobbly but seemed to at least be able to walk.

"Then I fight you, Bailey. You may shoot me, and that's fine. But maybe I'll still be able to get the gun from you and get away. Then I won't burn. Or maybe you kill me, but I die quickly and painlessly. Either way, are you willing to take that chance?"

Bailey cursed foully, pacing back and forth. Her need for vengeance won out. "Fine, she can go."

Joe didn't hesitate. He turned to Laura and began pushing her toward the door. Her eyes, still fuzzy and hazy from something akin to heatstroke, looked at him without much comprehension.

"Run toward the door, baby. There might be some fire, but just keep moving forward, okay? Crawl if you have to." He handed her his T-shirt. "Use this if you need it, to hold over your mouth."

She nodded. "You?"

Joe framed her face with both hands. He would've gladly spent the rest of his life with this woman. But knowing that she would live and have a life would be enough. "I'll be right behind you," he lied.

He kissed her. The sweetest, briefest of kisses. "I love you. Now run, okay?"

He turned her and pushed. She stumbled slightly then found her footing and ran wobbling toward the other side of the room.

Joe had to believe she would make it.

He picked the comm unit out of his pocket and put it back in his ear. "Steve? Anybody? If you can hear me, Laura is on her way out the front door. Send someone to help her. She's injured."

Joe looked up as Bailey turned her gun from him to where Laura was running.

"I've changed my mind. She can't live. If she lives you haven't suffered enough."

Joe ran toward Bailey but knew he would be too late to stop her from shooting Laura's retreating form in the back.

But out of the smoke stepped Steve Drackett. He shot Bailey before she could fire her gun. "I think you've caused quite enough people to suffer."

Bailey fell to the ground.

Steve walked forward and kicked the gun away from her hand.

At the sound of the gunshot Laura stopped and turned around. "Joe?"

"I'm here, sweetie." He ran over to her and put an arm around her. "Steve, let's go. This building is going to collapse any minute."

The smoke was already unbearable.

"She's still alive," Steve responded, gesturing to Bailey. "I'm going to carry her out."

Joe saw it at the same time Steve did. Bailey reached into her jacket pocket and pulled out a hand grenade.

Just like the one that had been used to kill Tyler. Bailey reached over with her other hand and pulled the pin.

"Grenade!" Steve yelled. "Get her out!"

Joe knew he wouldn't be able to get Laura to safety in the seconds they had. He saw Steve dive behind a wall in the other direction and dove with Laura back down into the false floor pulling the hatch closed over them. He wrapped the blanket around them and tucked Laura under him, shielding her as much as he could with his body.

A second later heat washed over them as well as an unbearably loud noise. Joe tightened his arms around Laura as everything went black.

LAURA TRIED TO figure out if she was dead.

It was the second time today she'd had to purposely use her brain, *force* it to work—something it usually did quite well on its own—to figure out if she was still alive or not.

She felt the same smothering heat she'd felt the first time. Unbearable heat that made breathing, moving, thinking, nearly impossible. Her breaths had come in short gasps, the effort forcing them further and further apart, until she'd been sure each breath had been her last.

Then she'd heard Joe's voice talking to Bailey.

Laura hadn't been able to make out what they were saying, but she knew he was nearby.

She'd held on. Her shoulders and feet and lungs wailed in agony but she'd held on because Joe had come for her.

But at some point she'd stopped even being able to focus on his voice.

The heat, the fumes from the gas Bailey had poured on her, had pulled her completely under.

But the next thing she knew Joe was there. Carrying her out of the hot hole of death. Shirtless. That didn't help her figure out if she was alive or not. Why wouldn't Joe have a shirt on if she was still alive?

Maybe she was in heaven.

It was just that everything had seemed so far away. Even Joe. Especially Joe.

She'd screamed in torture when he'd cut the bindings off her wrists and moved her shoulders, but no sound had come out. His fingers had helped her survive it.

The pain had let her know for sure she was alive, not in heaven.

Joe and Bailey had talked but Laura couldn't understand. Couldn't process.

Joe had wanted her to stand so she'd tried her best. Then he'd asked her to run, so she'd done that too.

But first he'd kissed her. He told her he loved her.

She wanted to stay with him. Wanted to kiss him more, but he'd told her to run.

She'd known something was wrong, but still couldn't get her brain to work enough to know what it was.

But as she lay here in the dark now, her brain figured out what it was.

Joe had made a deal with Bailey: he would die with her, if she would let Laura go. The bitch had reneged and tried to kill them both.

Joe had protected her by throwing them back in this hole and covering her with his body.

She was suffocating again, with Joe on top of her as well as the blanket. But this time her hands weren't tied; she could do something about it.

"Joe? Are you okay?"

He didn't answer. She twisted to her side, rolling him off her, and pulled the damn stifling material off them both.

Joe groaned and coughed.

It was the most beautiful sound Laura had ever heard.

Without his weight and the blanket on her, Laura could breathe more freely. There didn't even seem to be fire burning above them any longer.

"Are you okay?" she asked him again. Longer sentences still seemed beyond her.

"Yes. I think so. Are you?"

"My brain still hurts."

"You may have had a partial heatstroke from being trapped in that heat signature blocking material. It's not meant to be used indoors, or for extended periods of time."

Laura didn't like that. "Will my brain always be this slow?"

She couldn't see it, but she could hear Joe's smile. "I hope so. Then maybe I have a chance of keeping up with you."

Joe reached up with his legs and pushed against the hatch door. It didn't move. Then he touched the door with his hand. "It feels like Bailey's hand grenade actually saved us. It probably blew up so much of the roof of the building there wasn't enough to burn or suffocate us to death. It doesn't feel hot anymore, and the air seems cleaner."

"But we're trapped here."

"The team will be in here looking for us soon. We're not in any actual danger anymore. I just hope Steve made it out alive. I saw him dive the other way before the grenade went off."

Steve had been there, too. Laura's brain began to put pieces of information together. They lay there in silence while she figured it out, both of them content to just be with one another. Alive.

"You were going to let her kill you to get me out."

"Yes." Joe's voice was soft, husky.

"Why didn't you just fight her?"

"I couldn't take a chance you might get hurt in the process."

"Well, it was a terrible plan. Giving yourself over to die rather than take a chance fighting her."

Joe chuckled, wrapping an arm around her and pulling her closer. "How about next time a raging psychopath has us in her clutches I discuss the plan with you first and get approval."

"Yes. Better." She snuggled in to him. "Thank you."

"For getting you to approve the plan next time?"

"For keeping us both alive. For trusting that your team would have your back. For risking everything to find me."

"If you weren't here to share my life, it wasn't going to have much meaning anyway."

"Joe, I'm just afraid that—" She wanted to tell him she loved him. That she'd never stopped loving him. But that she was also scared that six months from now he would decide again she wasn't enough for him.

Being trapped in an enclosed space while a building burned down around them seemed like as good a place as any for that conversation.

But damn the Omega team for being so good at their job. Moments later they heard Joe's team calling for them.

"We'll finish this conversation soon, I promise." He kissed the side of her forehead before using his legs to kick up against the door to draw the team's attention.

Moments later the hatch opened. Steve stood there looking down at them.

"Joe with no shirt on and a beautiful woman in his arms. Seems about right."

Chapter Twenty-Four

Two weeks later Joe picked Laura up to take her on what he promised would be a "special lunch date."

Considering he'd been with her almost 24/7 since the incident with Bailey Heath, and that he'd taken her on a number of luxurious dates—including a couple on a private plane carrying them to Los Angeles and New York—she couldn't imagine what "special lunch date" meant.

She got into the car as he pulled up next to her law office building. "I can't miss any more work. I have to be back in no more than an hour."

He turned, tilted his head and gave her his most charming smile. "Hello to you, too, love." He reached over and kissed her.

Between the look and the kiss, every part of her body, and certain pieces of her clothing, just about melted. She sighed leaning into him.

"Sorry," she murmured against his lips. "I just can't afford to go flying across the country today. Work has been piling up."

She'd been hospitalized for complications stemming from heatstroke and fumes inhalation, including a seizure. The doctor had released her after just two days, but strongly suggested a couple of weeks of just low stress, fun activities.

Joe had taken two weeks' vacation from Omega and proceeded to escort Laura to all the places he loved. Places he'd always wanted to show her. Some were extravagant like the Four Seasons in Manhattan. But they also went to places like Sonny's Cafe in Galveston, Texas, a tiny hole-in-the-wall restaurant that he loved.

She had to admit, it had been fun. More. It had been lovely and peaceful and healing. Just what they both needed to put the nightmare of Bailey Heath behind them.

Joe's name had been cleared, of course. Although evidently there had been some other incident with the police involving Joe—Laura still didn't have all the details. But it had all been worked out.

The gossip sites had a field day with her and Joe's relationship. But after the story with Bailey was somehow leaked, and Laura was made out to be the heroine of the story, the sites seemed to take a different slant toward their relationship.

In every picture posted of the two of them Joe looked at her with such adoration, it was nearly impossible for the sites to say anything damaging about Laura without looking like fools. Joe's looks, his gestures, his movements toward Laura spoke volumes about his feelings.

But how long would they last? She forced herself not to think about tomorrows. Joe hadn't brought it up, so she didn't either.

"I promise to have you back in under an hour." He put the car in Drive and pulled away from her building.

"Okay, so where are we going for this 'special lunch date'?"

She'd barely gotten the question out before he pulled the car around the corner and parked it in a lot, then strode around to open her door for her.

They were at the county courthouse. Laura and her law partners had specifically chosen their office building because of its proximity to City Hall and the local courtrooms.

"What's going on? Oh my gosh, Joe, are you in trouble with the police again? You should've told me so I could be more prepared. What are the charges?"

She racked her brain trying to think of what charges could've been brought against Joe that would have him at the county courthouse rather than the criminal court downtown. This court was primarily used for real estate and marital purposes.

He gripped her elbow gently and led her up the stairs. "The general charge is being an idiot for too many years."

She couldn't help but laugh. "Well, in that case you really should've given me more time to prepare." He opened the door for her. "Seriously, what's going on?"

They went through security, Joe presenting his weapon to be held in a security box since he wasn't here on official business. "You'll figure it out in a minute. I enjoy being ahead of you for once."

They walked down the hall. "Figure what out? Joe, just tell me what's going on."

He stopped them in front of a courtroom door. "Get there faster, Laura. I know you can."

He twirled something around on the end of his pinkie as he said it.

A ring.

They were here to get married.

"Oh my God, Joe, we can't. It's too soon."

"Too soon? Hell, it's six years *too late*."

"But what about…" She trailed off unable to find the words she wanted.

"What about what?" He put his forehead against hers. "You need this so I can prove I'm not going to wake up one morning and change my mind again. I need this so I can have you legally bound to me while you're still slightly addled and will say yes."

"But—"

"I want you, Laura. I want you so badly I can't think straight for it. I love you so much that the thought of life without you causes me to break out in a panic."

"Are you sure?"

He cupped her face with both hands. "I have never been more sure of anything in my entire life." He kissed her. "We'll have a big wedding soon and invite everyone we know. We'll do this here today because I want you bound to me right now. Just you and me."

She nodded. He kissed her again and opened the door to the courtroom, his hand still gripping hers.

But when they walked in they realized they were not alone. Every member of the Critical Response team was already in the courtroom. She felt Joe's hand tighten around hers.

"You guys. How?" Joe basically sputtered.

Steve stepped forward. "You work for one of the most elite crime fighting agencies on the planet. Did you think we wouldn't discover the wedding of one of our own and be here to celebrate it?"

Joe wrapped his arm around Laura. "I guess not."

"Welcome to the family, Laura," Steve said.

Laura couldn't think of anywhere else in the world she'd rather be.

* * * * *